## DATE DUE

|  |  |
|---|---|
|  |  |
|  |  |
|  |  |
|  |  |
|  |  |
|  |  |
|  |  |
|  |  |
|  |  |
|  |  |
|  |  |
|  |  |
|  |  |
|  |  |
|  |  |
|  |  |

BRODART, CO.                    Cat. No. 23-221

D1559527

# KILL
## THE
# LION!

TEZONTLE

FONDO DE CULTURA ECONÓMICA
FUNDACIÓN PARA LAS LETRAS MEXICANAS
First Edition in Spanish (Siglo XXI), 1982
First Edition in English (FCE), 2008

Ibargüengoitia, Jorge
  Kill the Lion! / Jorge Ibargüengoitia ; translated by Helen Lane and
Ronald Christ. — México : FCE, f,l,m., 2008
  206 p. ; 21 × 14 cm — (Col. Tezontle)
  Original title: Maten al león
  ISBN 978-968-16-8610-9

  I. Mexican Literature — 20th Century I. Lane, Helen, tr. II. Christ,
Ronald, tr. III. Ser. IV. t.

LC PQ7298                                                  Dewey M863 I613k

This book was published with the assistance
of Fundación para las Letras Mexicanas, A. C.

Comments or suggestions: editorial@fondodeculturaeconomica.com
Visit our website and catalogue: www.fondodeculturaeconomica.com

Certified ISO 9001: 2000

Distribution in the entire American Continent

ISBN: 978-968-16-8610-9

Printed on acid-free paper by
Impresora y Encuadernadora Progreso, S. A. de C. V. (IEPSA)
Calzada San Lorenzo 244, 09830 México, D. F.
Printed in Mexico | Impreso en México

# KILL THE LION!

Jorge Ibargüengoitia

•

*Translated by*
Helen Lane
and
Ronald Christ

# Contents

The island of Arepa lies in the Caribbean Sea. An encyclopedic but abridged dictionary gives the following description: "Arepa is shaped like a perfect circle, thirty-five kilometers in diameter; 250,000 inhabitants, some Black, others White, and still others Guarupa Indians. It exports sugar cane and ripe pineapple. The capital is Puerto Alegre, where half the population lives. After fighting heroically for eighty-eight years, Arepa achieved its independence in 1898, when the Spanish withdrew for causes beyond their control. At present (1926) Arepa is a constitutional republic. Its president, Field Marshal don Manuel Belaunzarán, Boy Hero of the Wars for Independence and the last renowned survivor of those wars, is reaching the happy end of his fourth term in power, the maximum permitted him by law."

# 1. Catch of the Day

Nicolás Botumele, an old Black, skipper of a small Indian boat, goes out fishing as Nelson went to Trafalgar: standing in the stern, with one hand to his forehead and the stump of the other on the oar that serves him as a rudder, his good eye gazing across the milky morning sea. Facing him in the boat, two raggedy Blacks are paddling for him, and a kid, faking it. The fishing net, ready to be spread, lies in the prow.

The boat moves ahead on the flat sea. Nothing is heard but the splashing of the oars, the creaking of the rowlocks, and the straining of the rowers.

The skipper sights, in the distance, a school of fish. With a tug at the rudder, he changes direction and signals to the five Blacks watching him from the shore.

The boat is up on shore, beached. The fishermen, with their tattered pants dripping, are drawing in the trawl net. At the center of the net's arc, still in the water, the fish, highly agitated, try to escape. The skipper, in water up to his chest, herds them, untangling the folds of the net and gathering in the catch.

The fishermen pull with all their might. The belly of the net, brimful, comes up onto the beach and, still quivering, lies stretched out on the sand. The fishermen stand around the

bulge, looking at it hopefully, because it is enormous. Botumele tugs at the floats and exposes the swollen mass. Among
dying pompanos lies Dr. Saldaña's corpse. The fishermen observe the patent leather shoes, the gaiters, the English cashmere
jacket, and the mustache dripping seaweed.

The Puerto Alegre police have two mule-drawn vans. One
serves to transport policemen, the other to carry corpses or
prisoners.

The van for the dead, with a malarial coachman in the driver's seat, clears a path through the sellers of crullers and fried
fish and stops at the side door to the police headquarters. The
curious gather to watch how several policemen come out of
the headquarters, throw open the van's doors, and pull out the
stretcher from inside. A filthy blanket covers the bulge, not revealing anything more than the patent leather shoes and gaiters. The curious spectators crowd around and press hard in
order to see better.

"Make room, this isn't a show!" an official shouts.

Several policemen, brandishing clubs, move against the people, forcing them back and clearing a path along which policemen carrying the stretcher make their way. When the stretcher
disappears inside, the skirmish goes on between the police and
the onlookers.

A clumsy policeman gives a nasty blow to the back of a
Negro who gets away, and the club falls to the ground. Pereira,
a poor but clean-cut young man, who sees the incident and is
helpful, picks up the club and hands it to the policeman, who,
instead of thanking him, lights into him. Pereira is at first astonished, then grows frightened and, finally, raises the briefcase
he is carrying in his hand to protect his head. When he takes a
blow to his ribs, he breaks into a run and flees down the streets,

between walls covered with photographs of the dead man and posters that read: SALDAÑA FOR PRESIDENT. MODERATION.

Colonel Jiménez, with a Prussian uniform, a crew cut, and the look of a sinister Indian, tightly clutches the telephone in his private office.

"With the news, señor Presidente," he says, "that they've just brought in the corpse of the opposition candidate."

Field Marshal Belaunzarán, President of the Republic, Boy Hero, who was once handsome but has aged with the years, the worries of a statesman, women, and liters of Martell cognac consumed during twenty years in power, speaks into the telephone:

"Then investigate, Jiménez, and punish the guilty parties."

He hangs up the telephone, winking and pulling a devilish face at the man in front of him, on the other side of the large presidential desk.

"They've already found him."

Cardona, the vice-president, does not say a word. He has the same drooping moustache as the Marshal but is thin, bilious, and not very smart.

Belaunzarán gathers up the photographs taken during Saldaña's electoral campaign, as well as the texts of the speeches he gave, which cover the desk, throws them into the waste paper basket, and says:

"That's trash. Those worries are over and done with." He turns to Cardona and speaks to him with paternal sternness: "Now, Agustín, if you don't win this election, with no opponents in sight, it's because you're no good at politics—or anything else."

"Manuel, I'm doing everything possible," Cardona says in

all seriousness, never having seen the humor in the marshal's ironies.

"Well, I am too. Now I've gotten rid of your enemy. And with a little luck, we'll even finish off his party, because if things turn out as we've imagined them, the Moderates will wind up more discredited than my sainted mother."

He stands in front of the window and, through the glass, watches, on the other side of the Plaza Mayor, the idlers sitting in the Steamboat Café.

"I hope Jiménez does his duty and follows the trail we've left him," he says, before plunging back into his own thoughts.

In his chair, Cardona waits, patiently, to be told to leave.

Jiménez, between his desk and a portrait of Belaunzarán, dressed all in white and wrapped in the Arepa flag, says to Galvazo, his aide, who is in charge of investigations and tortures:

"We have to find out who killed Doctor Saldaña."

Galvazo is taken aback. He looks at his boss uncomprehendingly.

"It wasn't him?" He points at the portrait of the marshal.

Jiménez averts his gaze, squirms uncomfortably, and pretends not to have heard.

"The Marshal himself just gave me the order, Galvazo."

"All right, sir. We'll conduct an investigation."

A secretary, cadaverous and bored stiff, is typing, on a nickel-plated Remington, the deposition of Saldaña's chauffeur.

The basement of police headquarters is Galvazo's horror chamber. The procedure this man follows in order to obtain information is rudimentary, but infallible: it consists of forcing the interrogated men down on all fours and then yanking on their testicles until they talk.

Saldaña's chauffeur, tense and sweating, eyes downcast, tightens his belt and says:

"Last night, at 10 o'clock, I drove Doctor Saldaña to the house on San Cristóbal, number 3. He told me he didn't need me any more, and at that time I went home."

Galvazo and Jiménez, sitting on a table, their arms folded, listen to him. Galvazo turns to Jiménez and says to him, scandalized:

"Right in the middle of the election campaign, and he was visiting brothels! Such cynicism!"

The taking over of doña Faustina's house, the one at number 3 San Cristóbal, the most expensive brothel in Puerto Alegre, will be, from that moment on, part of Arepan mythology. The police entered through the front door, through the side door, through the back door, and through the second-floor windows, by means of the fire escape. They rounded up twenty hysterical whores in the Moorish room, laid hands on them, and took away the money they had earned by dint of so much work that evening a fortnight ago; afterward, they put them in the van for prisoners and made them spend the night in the clink, where three of them caught cold, and a jail sergeant, gonorrhea. The clients, except for the president of the Banco de Arepa, who reached safety by jumping out a window and breaking a leg, were booked, had their money extorted, and then were set free. It was futile for doña Faustina, the madam, to threaten Colonel Jiménez with telephoning the marshal.

Galvazo and Jiménez look around the deserted drawing room. The Gothic décor and the Moorish furniture, gallantly donated to the brothel by a libidinous millionaire, are turned topsy-turvy. A felt hat on the coat rack. Turning it around, Galvazo and Jiménez contemplate it like someone beholding a treasure: the hatband bears Saldaña's initials.

Saldaña's widow, swathed in suffocating veils, shows up at police headquarters in order to identify and claim, personally, her husband's body. She arrives accompanied by three of the deceased's best friends and political advisers: the Moderation deputies Bonilla, the most upright man in Puerto Alegre, as well as one of the richest; don Casimiro Paletón, civic poet and director of the Krauss Institute; and the Señor of the Network, who has no merits other than those of calling himself by that title and having served as a deputy.

Colonel Jiménez, in consideration of the deceased's civic virtues, invites the widow and her companions into his office, bids them sit down, and puts in front of the widow a receipt for the stabbed, split, disemboweled corpse, given in restitution so as to be stuffed and sewn up again. As the widow signs, an orderly enters carrying a package with the deceased's personal effects.

"All that's missing here are the doctor's hat, watch, and billfold," explains Jiménez, "which will be used as evidence at the trial."

The widow peers at him through the veils, and the other three, through their respective specs. None of them says a word.

"We expect to find out who the guilty parties are in a few hours," says Jiménez, uncomfortable.

The widow can put up with no more; she rises to her feet.

"A few hours? I've known who's guilty ever since I got the news. In order to apprehend him, all you need to do is go to the presidential palace."

The widow starts to sob. Don Casimiro goes over to her and pats her hand lightly. Bonilla stands up and approaches

Jiménez, whose hair is standing on end and who cannot hit on what to do. Bonilla says to him:

"The lady is broken up, Colonel. Don't pay any attention to what she's said."

The Señor of the Network looks out the window.

The widow goes on sobbing uncontrollably. Jiménez overcomes his confusion and says to Bonilla:

"Let's be very clear, Deputy: the motive was robbery and the culprits will be punished."

"Yes, Colonel."

Jiménez brings the meeting to an end by pointing to the sack that contains the patent leather shoes, etc. and saying to Bonilla:

"Take the sack."

Bonilla takes the sack, Jiménez goes to the door and opens it with a certain violence; he remains standing to one side, waiting for the others to leave the office. Don Casimiro Paletón leads the widow, who is still trembling, to the door; Bonilla follows them, carrying the sack, and the Señor of the Network leaves, bowing stiffly. When they have left, Jiménez shuts the door and, relieved, heaves a deep sigh.

The people accused of murdering Dr. Saldaña make up a sorry group: two whores, a faggot, and a couple of pickpockets. In his horror chamber, behind a railing, Galvazo lines them up and instructs them.

"In a minute you're going to be interviewed by the press. This is a privilege. Now each of you knows what you confessed to and what you have to say. If anybody louses up, we'll shoot you. Got it?"

The accused, terrified, say yes. Galvazo opens the door and in come the journalists.

# II. The Wake

Belaunzarán, in his shirtsleeves, is visiting the fighting cocks he keeps, caged, at his La Chacota villa. He talks foolishness to them, like an old maid to her canaries:

"What a pretty, pretty little cockie! What a pretty little beakie my cockie has!"

Agustín Cardona, dressed in strict mourning, enters the cockpit.

"I'm ready, Manuel," he says.

Belaunzarán turns round, folds his arms, studies Cardona from head to foot, and lets out a belly laugh.

"You look the very picture of grief. Nobody would guess you'd arranged the little job."

Cardona, who has no sense of humor, is offended.

"You ordered me to do it, Manuel," he says, weighed down with responsibilities.

"It had to be done, Agustín," the marshal responds, imitating him. He goes over to him, puts an arm around his shoulders, makes him to turn around, as they walk together toward the door, and says to him: "Can you imagine? What would we have done if our little doctor won the election? It would have been a national catastrophe. The return to Obscurantism."

Doctor Saldaña's body, powdered, with a topaz ring thrust onto his rigid hand, dressed in a jacket with its back seam unstitched, rests amidst the quilted padding of an ostentatious coffin.

At the four corners of the coffin, forming a pompous, soporific honor guard, stand Belaunzarán, Cardona, Bonilla, and Paletón.

The drawing room of the Saldaña house is large, dark, and full of the bereaved.

Belaunzarán stuffs two stubby fingers into his waistcoat pocket, takes out a gold watch, checks at the time, and puts the watch back. Instantly another four mourners come up to replace the guard.

Belaunzarán and Cardona depart together, walking toward the exit when a whispering, yet perfectly audible voice emerges from among the bereaved and declares:

"Assassin!"

Cardona continues on his way, with his heart pounding; Belaunzarán stops and turns to where the voice came from. He is facing Ángela Berriozábal, pretty, defiant, well dressed, ten centimeters taller than don Carlitos, her good-for-nothing husband, who is standing beside her.

Belaunzarán bows courteously and says:

"Good evening, doña Ángela."

Ángela, without responding, holds his gaze for a moment, then turns her back on him, brusquely, and starts walking away, disappearing among the mourners.

Belaunzarán, unperturbed, turns to don Carlitos, who shows a frozen smile, a red face. Belaunzarán smiles as well.

"Say good-night for me to your wife, it seems she hasn't seen me."

Don Carlitos is beside himself with gratitude.

"Absolutely certain that she hasn't seen you, señor Presidente!"

Belaunzarán says:

"Good-night," and walks out of the drawing room.

In the vestibule, a reporter, pencil and notebook in hand, stops him.

"Señor Mariscal, do you want to make a statement about the motive behind Dr. Saldaña's death?"

"Dr. Saldaña," says Belaunzarán, searching for eloquence, his gaze fixed on the wallpaper, "was a decent, irreproachable man. There are those who have the impression that he was my political rival. Not true. Our only difference lay in the fact that he was a member of the Moderate Party and I am a member of the Progressive Party. Our goal was the same: the good of Arepa. If I didn't back his candidacy it was because, Progressive that I am, I must support the candidate of my party, who is señor Agustín Cardona. Saldaña's death is an irreparable loss, not only for his supporters but also for the Republic. That's all."

Leaving the journalist struggling with his notes in his notebook, Belaunzarán goes to the door, where a servant hands him, between bows, his derby and walking stick.

The presidential Studebaker, with two murderers in the front seat and Cardona in a corner of the back, is parked outside Saldaña's house. Belaunzarán, with the derby on his head and the walking stick in his hand, gets into the car. Before closing the car door, he says to Cardona, in a cruel jest:

"You ran like a rabbit!"

"What would you like me to do, Manuel?"

"To stand your ground, Agustín! They meant you when they said 'assassin'."

The car takes off. Cardona, bilious, looks out the window. Belaunzarán recollects, satisfied:

"But it all turned out fine. I decided to cover your retreat. I confronted her, and I sent her fleeing. That woman's got bigger balls than her husband . . . Not to mention those present."

Cardona, unresponsive, looks out the car window.

Belaunzarán takes off his derby and jacket, loosens his necktie.

"To avoid trouble, and this kind of accusation, we'll have to make the trial look real. It'll be necessary to shoot one or two of the accused. The judge must get his orders. You'll take care of that tomorrow."

Cardona looks at him, annoyed.

"But how are we going to shoot them, Manuel? When we promised them protection!"

"Yes, but nobody knows that, Agustín!"

A dense crowd fills the cockpit. The rancid sweat of two hundred men in addition to their alcoholic breath mingles with the smoke from the cigars they are smoking. The faces are of every color, from the jet black of the Negroes and the liverish green of the Guarupa Indians to the vermillion red of the Galicians. The uproar is deafening.

The gamecocks peck, hop, flap, bleed. Around them, outside the enclosure, moving in nervous circles, absorbed in the fight, walk Belaunzarán, with his celluloid collar open and twisted, scarcely held down by the button in back, his shirt soaked, and a poor breeder of fighting cocks, shoeless, clothes patched, wearing a woven palm hat.

Belaunzarán's cock slits the throat of the other bird, which is transformed into a gush of blood and a pile of feathers. The uproar grows louder.

Belaunzarán goes over to the spot where his bird stands, picks him up from the ground as though he were made of porcelain, presses him against his chest, looks at him with tender pride, skillfully detaches the razor-sharp gaff, and puts the bird back in his cage. Satisfied, he takes out a white linen handkerchief and wipes dry his sweating face and the nape of his neck. Several bookies come into the ring and give him his winnings. An assistant, malevolent and uniformed, carries the cage; Belaunzarán, money in hand, comes over to the breeder, who is picking up his favorite bird by the scruff of its neck, and hands him some bills. The breeder receives them hat in hand.

Upon seeing the magnanimous gesture, the raucous, boozy crowd fills with vulgar sentimentality and, with tears in the eyes, shouts: "Viva Mariscal Belaunzarán!"

And Belaunzarán walks out of the ring in triumph, as after his greatest battles, and reaches the spot where Cardona is waiting for him; in a sour mood, the vice-president helps him stuff the money into the sack.

# III. By Way of a Burial

The next day will be historic for the Arepan Republic. The landowners, businessmen, professionals, artisans, and maids from good houses are burying Dr. Saldaña and, with him, their hopes for Moderation. The farmers, fishermen, stevedores, greasy-food vendors, and beggars arrive at the palace tumultuously, dancing the conga, and asking, in chorus, that Belaunzarán accept, for the fifth time, and contrary to what is provided in the Constitution, the presidential candidacy.

But what is most important takes place in the Chamber of Deputies. The session starts at 9:00 A.M. with all ten deputies in attendance and with a minute of silence, as a sign of mourning for the death of the opposition's candidate. At 10:30, Deputy Bonilla requests permission, in the name of the Moderates, to withdraw in order to attend the burial of Dr. Saldaña. The President of Debates grants permission, with the provision that, as is customary in such cases, the remainder of the assembly continue, with plenary powers. Since the Moderates are punctilious people who would not miss a burial and since there are only matters of no interest on the agenda, Bonilla, Paletón, and the Señor of the Network, in strict mourning and with long faces, leave the chamber. When they are scarcely getting into the car that will take them to the burial, Deputy Borunda requests, for circumstances beyond their control, that the agenda be changed and they proceed to discuss Article 14, having to do with electoral regulations. The request is approved, and at 11:05, as the Moderates are filling the deceased's home, the Chamber, in full session, approves, by seven votes to zero, the deletion of the paragraph stating: "Shall remain in office for a maximum of four terms and shall not be re-elected for the fifth time."

The Krauss Institute, the island's highest center of learning and a bastion of Arepan wisdom, is located in a stone building, begrimed and musty, that had been a convent. In the cloister's corridors, where once walked nuns, gossiping or reciting the rosary, now walk the adolescent sons of millionaires, wearing short pants, picking their noses, and preparing themselves to enter Harvard or the Sorbonne.

Salvador Pereira, drawing teacher by necessity and amateur violinist, enters a classroom, briefcase in hand. Twenty students sitting with their legs wide apart look at him insolently.

Pereira opens the briefcase on the desk and takes out some T-squares.

"In today's class," he explains, "we are going to learn how to use the T-square."

Tintín Berriozábal, the handsomest student and biggest idler in the whole school, rises to his feet and starts to speak without waiting for permission.

"Teacher, are you patriotic?"

Pereira, disconcerted, looks at Tintín before speaking.

"Of course."

"Then we shouldn't have class. Today Dr. Saldaña is being buried."

A chorus of plaintive voices is heard, pleading:

"Yes, teacher, let us go!"

Pereira smacks the desk with the T-squares, demanding silence. When he gets it, he declares:

"We are in mechanical drawing. Political events do not concern us. Today we are going to learn how to use the T-square."

Another chorus is heard, begging:

"Teacher, don't be mean, let us go!"

Pereira strikes again with the T-squares and, amid the din, commands:

"Silence! Silence! Silence!"

In silence, with the hearse leading, the horses draped in mourning, the coachman wearing a high hat, Dr. Saldaña's funeral cortege moves forward, slowly and majestically, toward the mausoleum.

Behind the hearse, in black clothes, walk the rich men of Arepa; after the rich men come their cars, with their wives inside; and after the cars, the poorest of Dr. Saldaña's supporters.

In the Berriozábal's seven-seat Dion-Button, Ángela, Saldaña's widow, and doña Conchita Parmesano, in mourning and sweating, with dark circles of sleeplessness under their eyes, drink coffee from nickel-plated glasses, filled from a Thermos, and say nothing.

Fausto Almeida, raised up over the fence, dressed in dirty white, with greasy hair falling over his mulatto forehead, shouts himself hoarse:

"For twenty years Mariscal Belaunzarán has protected the rights of the poor. For twenty years he has led this country along the path of progress. We beg him not to abandon us. We beg him to accept a fifth candidacy."

A crowd of unemployed men shouts enthusiastically. Almeida leaps down from the wall and breaks into a run toward the presidential palace, and the rabble follows him, to the beat of congas and *bodoleques*, drums and *rungas*.

Professor Pereira, holding the T-squares to the blackboard, expertly draws parallel lines. At his back all is chaos. The whole class, except for Pepino Iglesias, the half-blind student, who is at his desk in the first row, asleep behind the thick lenses of his glasses, is leaning out the window, waiting for the funeral cortege.

Pereira turns around and becomes furious, pounds on the desk, awakens Pepino, and shouts:

"I told you, this is a drawing class: take your seats!"

The students, taking their time, go back to their places and Pereira to his T-squares.

The door opens and don Casimiro Paletón, director of the institute, comes in. The whole class rises noisily because their belt buckles catch on the lids of the desks.

Don Casimiro Paletón looks at Pereira sternly.

"Professor Pereira, what are you waiting for? What are you thinking about? This is a day of national mourning. Let the boys go so they can accompany Dr. Saldaña's funeral cortege, which will soon pass in front of the institute."

"All right, señor Director," says Pereira, abashed.

Paletón turns to the boys:

"Boys, never forget this day. The death of Dr. Saldaña is the greatest catastrophe that ever happened in Arepa."

That said, he hastily withdraws, moved to tears by his own eloquence.

Once the door is shut, the boys' happiness explodes: they shout, laugh, bang wastebaskets, grab their books, and take off at a run. They leave Pereira alone, grimacing in annoyance, putting the T-squares back into his briefcase.

Saldaña's funeral cortege left from his house on Paseo Nuevo, went down Espolón to Cordobanes, turned left, proceeded along Manga de Clavo, and there, upon passing in front of the Krauss Institute, bumped into the *Belaunzaranista* demonstration that had started out as a pep rally on Llanos del Cigarral, then scared off the flies at the San Antonio dump, grew stronger in the Fishers Market, squeezed together amid the streets of the old city, and ended up in front of the palace, having turned into a clamor for the dictatorship.

On finding itself in front of the Krauss Institute, the cortege and the demonstration come to a halt; the horses are nervous, the coachman uncertain, the rich men fearful that the screeching crowd will cover them with spit. The poor people, for their part, on seeing before them the black hearse with the deceased inside, also come to a halt, looking dismayed, and silencing their mouths as well as their musical instruments. For a moment, nobody moves in the street full of people. No longer are horses' hoofs heard striking against worn paving stones. Pereira appears at a window of the Krauss Institute and looks at those two motionless streams. The sun is directly overhead, there is not a breath of air, the flies renew their microscopic hunting.

In the end, superstition gains the upper hand. The poor remove their palm hats, the coachman lashes the horses and makes them go forward, the poor separate and make way for the hearse, the rich close ranks and start walking, convinced they are going to get nits, the elegant cars move ahead with a string of farts.

Dr. Saldaña, head of his army of no-accounts, crosses, like Moses, a pestilential and divided Red Sea in order to arrive at the cemetery.

When the cortege has passed by, the crowd dons their hats,

the small drums sound, the people shout and surge forward, hopping up and down and singing:

*Let me tell you, nothing will stop*
*Belaunzarán*

In the palace's Green Room, with a chandelier, Empire-style tapestries and furniture acquired by a megalomaniac captain general from the time of Queen Isabela (of Spain), are seated Mr. Humbert H. Humbert, Sir John Phipps, and M. Coullon, ambassadors of the United States, His British Majesty, and France, respectively, smoking Partagás cigars that the chief of protocol has just offered them.

In the Reception Chamber, Belaunzarán receives the deputies, who come to give him word of the law they have just modified. Borunda is the spokesman:

"Señor Presidente, you are free to accept the candidacy."

The marshal, playing the shirker, raises the palms of his hands modestly:

"But, boys, I'm already very tired."

Cardona, who is watching his hopes go up in smoke, makes a vinegary face.

Outside, the mob's singing can be heard. Chucho Sardanápolo, minister of Public Welfare, and the chief superintendent of the palace, come in to ask Belaunzarán:

"Go out onto the balcony, señor Presidente, the people are expecting you."

In the Plaza Mayor, the organized commoners sing in a mulatto rhythm:

*Belaunzarán*
*Don't you leave us*
*Belaunzarán*

*Oh, no no no*
*Don't you leave us*
*Belaunzarán*

Belaunzarán, from the balcony, weeps emotional tears, and thanks the festive crowd. Acknowledging the festivity, he nods yes and, seeing that, the people explode joyously, and the revelry continues.

Belaunzarán steps in from the balcony.

In the Reception Chamber, among deputies and ministers, stands Cardona, sour-faced as usual, with his shoulders drooping as never before. Belaunzarán enters the chamber, crosses over to Cardona, hugs him, and says, his voice pompous with emotion:

"Forgive me, Agustín, but I can't deny them anything. Another time."

Belaunzarán steps away from Cardona, leaving him to stare at the carpet and all the others to look at him regretfully, and then the marshal exits through the door opening onto the corridor leading to his private office.

In his office, Belaunzarán changes. The emotion and reserve desert him. He quickens his step, goes around the grand desk, pulls out a chair, passes by his statue, and opens the bathroom door, unfastening the buttons of his fly.

In the Green Room, the ambassadors are growing bored, staring into space. The noise from the bathroom arouses them from their self-absorption. They prick up their ears, stand erect, twist their necks to see who is entering.

Belaunzarán, turning his back on the artificial waterfall he has just caused and that continues to gush, is standing on the threshold, buttoning his fly and smiling graciously:

"Gentlemen, I'm at your service."

KILL THE LION!

That said, he sits down in a chair slightly higher than those the ambassadors occupy.

Mr. Humbert H. Humbert, plump and glib, straining to be pleasant, takes the floor between smiles and ambiguous vowels:

"My colleagues present here and I come to tell you that our respective governments will look favorably on your continuing in power, considering that you are a statesman like no other."

"Thank you very much," Belaunzarán says.

Sir John Phipps, old and withered, not understanding Spanish and deaf, smiles amiably at Belaunzarán, and nods his head affirmatively, wishing, deep down inside, that what Humbert H. Humbert has said were what he would like to have said. M. Coullon, round and with a big head, his face full of reproaches, makes no gesture whatsoever and fixes his gaze on the greyhounds in the tapestry hanging in front of him. During his twenty years as ambassador in these Indian lands, he has never succeeded in making himself understood to anyone, reflecting the fact that, given French's being the diplomatic language, there is no reason to use any other.

"As for the Law of Expropriation and the Agriculture Program you have proposed, my dear Marshal," Humbert goes on, smiling more than ever, "we are in agreement that they will not harm any foreign interests, nor will they be an obstacle to Arepa's meeting its obligations, which have been contracted with our governments, isn't that so?"

"That is so, Mr. Humbert," Belaunzarán says, smiling slightly and glancing briefly into the eyes of each one of his visitors, so as to convey his sincerity.

The Anglo-Saxons smile at Belaunzarán benevolently. Coullon grumbles in French:

"*Bien!*"

# IV. Private Life

Salvador Pereira, wearing a driver's cap and a Palm Beach suit, both gifts, the briefcase under his arm, selects the smallest among the dead porgies on the fish store's table. First, he fingers the fish to see if it is firm, then he looks into its blind eyes, and, finally he smells it. Satisfied with the results of these operations, he puts the fish on the counter, in front of the fishmonger, who cleans it, brushes it, and wraps it in newspaper. Pereira pays and puts the package in his briefcase, between the T-squares and a Schubert sonata.

In the shade of an almond tree, Pereira watches a streetcar approaching out of the distance, lurching from side to side, creaking, coming to a stop with a rattle, starting up with a groan, and bearing a sign in front that reads: PAREDÓN, as well as an advertisement for The Red Boot, importers of American and European footwear. Pereira leaps aboard, with all the agility and experience of his twenty-five years as a very poor man.

In her mother's living room, Esperanza, Pereira's wife, gloomy and disheveled, is sewing clothes for somebody else amid the percale curtains, the wicker furniture, the Congo-yellow painted floor, an image of the Sacred Heart, the wedding photograph, and the colored print showing some cupids rowing the gondola of a fat Venus. In the kitchen, doña Soledad, owner of the house and Pereira's mother-in-law, is sweating, getting upset from thinking about the chasm between having and not having a cook, and watching over the black beans boiling in a clay pot.

Pereira comes into the house, greets his wife with an unenthusiastic kiss that is not returned, hangs his jacket and cap on the tusks of a cardboard wild boar, goes to the corner where his music stand reposes, takes up the violin, opens the score, and gets ready to play, when Esperanza says to him:

"You haven't asked me how I'm feeling."

"How are you feeling?"

"Really bad. My liver's hurting me again."

"Go see a doctor."

"I don't have the money."

"Drink some yerba santa."

"It doesn't help me."

"Then pray to the Sacred Heart."

He plays a note, tunes the violin, starts playing again. Doña Soledad comes in, waving a grease-stained Japanese fan, her hair stuck to her sweating brow.

"Did you forget the fish again or did you spend the money on something else?"

Pereira, not rude, docile, sets down the violin, goes over to the briefcase, takes out the package and hands it to his mother-in-law, who walks out of the room, unwrapping the porgy, sniffing it suspiciously.

Pereira goes back to playing. At the second note, he realizes that Esperanza is crying silently. He lowers the violin and asks, concerned:

"What's wrong?"

Esperanza covers her mouth with a handkerchief and sobs. She suddenly rises, like someone, unable to contain herself, who does not want to make a spectacle of herself, and goes to the door, saying, between sobs, a dripping nose, and the handkerchief she holds over her mouth:

"It's just that we're so poor!"

She walks out, slamming the door, and in the privacy of her bedroom, flings herself stomach down on the brass bed on which have cohabited, peacefully, three generations of women embittered by the social failure of their respective husbands.

Pereira opens the door and, standing in the doorway, sees, disconsolately, the way his wife's buttocks tremble as she sobs. He enters the room, shuts the door, sets the violin on a chair, and with a tragic face, makes a leap onto Esperanza and nips the nape of her neck. Tearful, she says: "No, no, no," but allows him to squeeze her breasts.

Pereira, after intercourse, plays the violin with inspiration and bad taste. At his side, Esperanza sews calmly, her eyes lowered.

Pereira, Esperanza, and Soledad, sitting silently at the table after dinner, drink black coffee, looking, with a certain nostalgia, at the porgy's skeleton lying on a chipped plate.

Pereira, in the afternoons, goes to the beach in his shirtsleeves, and sits for hours, squatting, motionless, with his hands above his eyebrows, making a sunshade for his eyes as they gaze at the empty horizon.

At night, lighting his way with an oil lamp, Pereira plays chess, cautiously, with the Terror of the Police Station, Pedro Galvazo, in his mother-in-law's house. Soledad, Esperanza, and Rosita Galvazo, sitting in wicker rocking chairs, out on the street, take the fresh air, scratch at the tangles in their hair, fan themselves, and cast doubt, shrilly, on their neighbors' virtue.

Pereira advances a rook and says:

"Checkmate."

Galvazo, flushed and agitated, pounds the mahogany table, painted blue, with his fist, knocks over his queen and says:

"I'm screwed to the eyeballs."

Pereira, on the defensive, cornered in his chair, hopes that his opponent's rage will cool down. From between the curtains drifts in doña Rosita Galvazo's stupid voice:

"I'm telling you it's true, she dresses her husband in short skirts."

Soledad and Esperanza laugh delightedly and deny the gossip, wanting to know all the details.

Galvazo, under control, assumes the role of a good loser and says, magnanimously:

"That was a shitty match, Pereira, my friend."

Pereira grows calm, nods in agreement and smiles timidly.

The Berriozábal house was built at the beginning of the century, with money from don Carlitos's father and the talent of an Italian architect who became a millionaire on his trips through the uncivilized countries. In the circular drive, beneath the shade of the date palm and visible to everyone, stand the family's cars—the convertible Dussemberg and the Dion-Button sedan.

Ángela, who has a weakness for the arts, has transformed the shaded passageway communicating with the interior parquet into a music room, with large windows opening onto the green lawn, the magnolia tree, the poinsettias, the jacaranda trees, the rubber tree, the roses of Castile, and the peacocks.

On Wednesday afternoons the most refined souls of Puerto Alegre gather in this room to play good music badly and to listen to don Casimiro Paletón's manly verses as well as to delicately passionless lines by Pepita Jiménez, an amateur poet.

Tintín Berriozábal, reclining on the chintz-covered sofa,

rests his head on his mother's legs, which are still firm, as she strokes his hair.

"Your friend, Professor Pereira," Tintín says, "is an idiot."

"He's not my friend, he's a guest. He plays the violin admirably. He's an essential part of the quintet. Whether he's an idiot or not, I don't care one way or the other. Get up, you're wrinkling my dress."

"I don't feel like it."

Ángela goes on stroking, peacefully, her son's hair, as she says severely:

"Don't be disrespectful."

Among the azaleas, the vinylicas, fasceshias, and pergolias of Pergamon, Ángela, in a white dress, points out to the Black gardener which flowers he should cut and give to the maid, who is coming for them with a bouquet in her arms.

Don Carlitos, dressed in white, with a Cardiff collar, a British tie held in place by a pearl tiepin, and two-tone shoes, appears on the footpath and inquires, jokingly:

"And is food not served in this house?"

He goes over to his wife and, rising slightly on his heels, brushes his mustache, close trimmed and gray, across his wife's cheek. She looks at him without interest.

"Those shoes are terrible."

"They look terrible to you? I like them."

With an owner's pride he places a hand on his wife's firm buttock so that the servants see that he still can. She says, under her breath:

"Don't touch me."

Don Carlitos pretends to realize, only then, that they are not alone, says "Ah!" takes his hand away, and walks beside his wife a few steps down the path. The gardener and the maid exchange a split-second, bored glance.

KILL THE LION!

Don Carlitos cuts a medlar and eats it.

"At the casino they say it's a fact. We have Belaunzarán with us for another five years. Unless we come up with a brilliant idea."

"Such a disgrace!" Ángela exclaims.

Don Carlitos adopts a stern tone:

"Disgrace or no disgrace, I'm going to ask that you don't call him an assassin again. We've got to be diplomatic and protect our properties."

Ángela turns to the gardener and says to him:

"Cut three of the rose of Castile."

The gardener sets to work; Ángela watches him; don Carlitos spits out the pit and eats another medlar. He drops his stern tone and tries to make her listen to reason:

"Besides, the man's in the best of moods. I'm playing dominoes with him today."

"Do whatever you like," says Ángela, sniffing a rose.

Don Carlitos spits out the second pit and says:

"All right, at what time do we eat around here?"

"Right now. The bouquet is ready. We'll eat, and you'll get there on time for your appointment with the bandit."

Don Carlitos turns supplicant again:

"Ángela, please: be sensible."

"Don't worry, I won't say again what I think."

Preceded by the maid, they both start back to the house. Don Carlitos, in good humor, eats another medlar.

"You won't regret it," he says, still sucking.

"I need another suit for Pereira," Ángela says, "the Palm Beach you gave him is threadbare already."

Don Carlitos raises his eyebrows, feigning outrage.

"But what does that man do with his clothes?"

"He wears them. He hasn't got another suit."

"Give him that pinstripe I never liked, and tell him that if I dress him, it's not so he can give my son bad grades."

"Your son's a loafer."

"All the more reason. You return love with love."

They go into the house together.

# v. The Arepa Casino

During the last third of the previous century and at the beginning of the present one, Arepa's rich people built their houses on Paseo Nuevo. Some, the landowners, came from the island's interior, fleeing the bandits; and others, the merchants, from the city's center, fleeing the bad smells.

Paseo Nuevo is three blocks long, with a view of the sea and a median strip with tamarinds, jacarandas, laurels, and magnolias between the paved-over arroyos. There, among gardens and wrought-iron gates, stand the houses of the Berrio-zábals, the Redondos, and the Regalados, the island's most powerful tycoons. Some houses call to mind the Taj Mahal, others, the Córdoba Mosque, and still others, the baroque palace of some Bohemian nobleman.

With the exodus to Paseo Nuevo, some of the rambling old mansions at the city's center were left vacant. In one of those, the former home of the Verdegollos, was established the Arepa Casino, whose members include all those who have self-respect, are respected, and have the money to pay the dues.

The casino, founded so that the island's gentlemen would have a place to pass their time playing cards and reading back issues of periodicals, was converted, thanks to pressures exerted by rampant Progressivism, into the Moderate Party's meeting place and base of operations.

On the night of the day that Dr. Saldaña was buried, a stormy meeting took place in the auditorium. Nobody remembered to mourn the deceased, and everybody to reproach the three deputies for their bad idea of leaving the Chamber in order to attend the funeral, leaving the field to the Progressives.

"We're lucky it didn't give them time to approve the Law of Expropriation," commented don Carlitos, and that was the kindest thing said at the meeting.

The Law of Expropriation, which has been held up in the Chamber for fifteen years owing to the Moderates' opposition, provides that all properties belonging to Spaniards and to the sons of Spaniards, that is, to all property owners on Arepa, will come under state control.

"The moment has come to close up shop and clear out of here for somewhere else," said don Ignacio Redondo, for the $n^{th}$ time in fifteen years.

But the target of the insults, more than the deputies, was an absent member, the marshal, who was accused of playing dirty under the table.

"And I, who called him Boy Hero in one of my best poems!" exclaimed don Casimiro Paletón, raising one hand to his brow.

"It was a youthful indiscretion," said Barrientos, consoling him, while walking on crutches from his accident at doña Faustina's place two nights ago.

They agreed to meet again, with calmer minds and the object of determining who was going to be the Party's presidential candidate to replace Saldaña and confront El Gordo Belaunzarán, if not with high hopes, at least with dignity.

The second meeting got off to a bad start, opening already closed wounds. Bonilla, who had been passed over once before, when everybody chose Saldaña, and who felt himself to be one of the most viable candidates, by virtue of being "the most upright man in Arepa," was offended when Coco Regalado, a young carouser, commented that integrity is not a civic virtue. "We've put up with twenty years of government by bandits, and nobody has found fault with them," he says to support his argument.

Bonilla, who is up on the platform, thrusts out his jaw, lengthening his face, and, without opening his mouth, glances over those present, as though saying to them:

"Just look what we've come to. What must the younger generations think?"

To most of them the statement appears cynical, but with quite a bit of underlying truth.

"The Blacks like slick guys," says don Bartolomé González, the most realistic one in the group. "And Blacks are the ones who win elections."

Everyone pulls a "sad-but-true" face. Paco Ridruejo, a serious young man from a good family, asks to speak and says:

"I propose Cussirat."

The meeting turns lively. The discussions start. Pepe Cussirat, "the first civilized Arepan," in the memorable phrase of *El Mundo*'s reporter, Armando Duchamps, has been abroad for fifteen years, studying at the best universities.

"He's got something no one has seen in Arepa; namely, culture," says Ridruejo.

"One moment!" pleads Bonilla, who is personally offended, and rightfully so: "Here we have don Casimiro Paletón, who is a fountain of knowledge."

Don Casimiro, who is on the platform, next to Bonilla, modestly lowers his eyes and, smiling tolerantly, says:

"Yes, but Cussirat is younger."

Barrientos, supporting himself on his crutches and one good leg, rises to his feet in order to declare:

"I approve this idea. We need a candidate who's not one of us, who are very much in the public eye. We need new faces, and Cussirat's is one of them."

"Besides not being one of us," says don Bartolomé González, as an irrefutable argument, "Cussirat is one of ours."

Don Bartolomé is one of the Rolls Royce Gonzálezes, so called to distinguish them from the other Gonzálezes, who do not have a Rolls.

"Cussirat rides horses, he has a plane, plays golf, hunts deer, and speaks three languages. What more do we want?" Paco Ridruejo enumerates.

"And he's thirty-five years old!" exclaims don Remigio Iglesias, one of the oldest Moderates. "If this Party is to save itself, it'll be with young people."

"And nobody remembers him!" somebody says.

"He's got no skeletons in the closet!"

"Lack of support could be a drawback," warns the Señor of the Network, who has never been outside Arepa.

"He's one of those who fled because he couldn't pull his bacon out of the fire," comments don Ignacio Redondo, forgetting the million he has in Spain's Banco de Bilbao. "They didn't stay, like us, to confront the situation."

When Belaunzarán invented the Law of Expropriation, the Cussirat family, who were filthy rich, sold properties, invested in New York, and went to live abroad with no intention of returning.

Paco Ridruejo swears that during the three weeks he spent with Cussirat in White Plains, there was not a day when the man did not think back on Arepa.

"He's very nostalgic about his country," he ends by saying.

"The Cussirats are, and always have been, great friends of

my family," says Don Carlitos, "but, if Pepe comes into power, will he look out for our interests?"

"As though they were his own!" swears Ridruejo.

Partly because of the enthusiasm always provoked by an idea where none had previously existed, and partly because of the lack of any other solution, the Moderates that night endorsed inviting Cussirat to be their candidate. In their resolution it was stated, as well as expressed in the letter sent to Cussirat, that they had reached this decision, "in consideration of his lofty civic virtues, the stringency of his political position, reflected in the voluntary exile he has imposed on himself, as well as his personal merit."

In reality, one of the factors that won the battle was expressed by Bartolomé González, in an optimistic, visionary moment:

"If he comes in by plane, we'll win the election."

Because in Arepa no one had ever seen an airplane.

KILL THE LION!

# VI. High Life

Ángela, holding on to the enormous Bossendorffer piano her husband bought at auction; Dr. Malagón, shaking his shock of gray hair, half rising from his chair in order to play louder, out of tune and executing flourishes on the violin; Pereira, playing his part very timidly; old Quiroz, gloomy at the viola; and Lady Phipps, the cello between her parted legs, revealing her underwear and elevating her strong chin—the great Lecumberri quintet plays furiously.

Don Casimiro Paletón, waiting for the moment to read his "Ode to Democracy," which he has just finished composing; Conchita Parmesano, dunking British biscuits in sherry; Father Inastrillas, dozing; Pepita Jiménez, racked with aesthetic emotion; Barrientos, having pursued his hostess's favors for the past five years and not taking his eyes off her now; the two Regalado sisters, bored; don Gustavo Anzures, attending because he did not go to the Casino—all seated on Viennese chairs, making up the audience.

The piece culminates in a sublime, out-of-tune chord. The listeners burst into applause and "Bravos!"

"What a fantastic concert!" exclaims doña Conchita, shaking off the crumbs.

"What would become of us without you, doña Ángela!" says Father Inastrillas, waking up. "This island would be a wasteland."

Barrientos, limping and twiddling his mustache, comes close to Ángela and, looking into her eyes, says:

"Magnificent!"

Malagón, with his impassioned Catalan gestures, tells Pereira, sputtering:

"You didn't follow me. That's not the way the second movement's played. When I go *taraliralirali*, you ought to go *tiraliraliralá* and not *taraliralirali* the way you did, because then I can't do the *taralalitaralalá*, which is what comes next. Understand?"

"Yes, Doctor, I'll try to do it better next time."

"This music," says Pepita Jiménez, accepting the dessert glass of orange sherbet offered by a servant, "is so marvellous it depresses me."

"*I say!*" remarks Lady Phipps, putting her cello aside and closing her legs.

Old Quiroz puts his viola away in its case without uttering a word.

"You people are at the level of the best orchestras," says don Casimiro Paletón, dousing his whiskers.

Don Carlitos comes into the room, dressed in the English manner and full of good humor.

"Am I late?" he asks.

"You don't know what you've missed!" says don Gustavo Anzures.

"You're in time to hear the ode don Casimiro's going to read us," says Ángela.

"I'm delighted! Delighted!" exclaims don Carlitos, resigned.

"It's an improvisation," Paletón warns modestly.

"I was delayed because I was playing dominoes with Belaunzarán," don Carlitos explains to don Gustavo Anzures, discretely. "Apples or oranges, you have to be on good terms with everybody. I asked him not to expropriate my estate in Cumbancha."

"Intercede for me, don Carlitos! Remember, I'm a landowner too," Anzures begs him. "I'll appreciate it."

"Wait. Right now's too soon. You have to be well placed to make the leap. But, as soon as there's a proper moment, count on me."

Ángela approaches Pereira and tells him, discretely kind: "I have a suit for you."

Pereira, overwhelmed with appreciation, says:

"Thank you, señora!"

"Soon as don Casimiro reads his ode, I'll give it to you. Remind me."

"Of course, señora."

Ángela, looking at Pereira's shoes, coming apart at the seams, asks him:

"What's your shoe size?"

At that moment, a servant enters and delivers a cablegram on a tray to Ángela. General silence. Expectation. Ángela raises a hand to her breast, as though to prevent her heart from leaping out.

"What can it be?" she asks, looking at the envelope in fascination.

"Well, open it, dear, and see what it says inside," says don Carlitos coming closer, full of curiosity. "Quick, you've got us on tenterhooks!"

Ángela opens the cablegram and reads it. Her face lights up. She raises her eyes and says to the gathering:

"Good news for everyone! It's from Pepe Cussirat. He says: I ACCEPT COMMA IN PRINCIPLE COMMA THE NOMINATION PERIOD I WILL ARRIVE BY AIRPLANE PERIOD CUSSIRAT."

While Ángela presses the cablegram to her breast, enthusiastic cries are heard from several of those present.

KILL THE LION!

"Bravo!" says Barrientos.

"The boy's a treasure!" says don Carlitos.

"My ode will not be called 'To Democracy' but 'To Cussirat.' Although it must be noted that by rights this cablegram ought to have been addressed to the Moderate Party at its official address, which is the Arepa Casino."

Don Carlitos explains:

"A very close friendship has always bound us to Pepe. It's quite natural that he wanted us to be the first to know his decision."

First, the sound of a glass shattering is heard, then a dull thud, as of a falling package. The orange sherbet that Pepita Jiménez had been eating is now staining the Persian carpet, alongside the lifeless body of the poetess.

While Dr. Malagón examines her, Conchita Parmesano pats her lightly with a rigid hand and explains to Padre Inastrillas, who is at her side, ready to administer Extreme Unction:

"Pepe Cussirat was her fiancé. She's been waiting for him for fifteen years. Naturally, she fainted, the poor thing."

Pepita Jiménez opens her eyes and asks:

"Where am I?"

Dr. Malagón discharges her.

"It was the emotion, a little cognac and she'll be all right."

The fright passes. Don Carlitos leaves the room, calling out:

"A cognac!"

Somebody remarks: "What a scare you gave us, Pepita!"

Pereira touches Ángela's arm as she holds a scented handkerchief to Pepita's nostrils and says:

"Size twenty-six shoes."

Nighttime. Pereira enters the dark living room of his mother-in-law's house carrying in his arms the violin case, the briefcase with the music, the pinstripe suit, and the two-toned shoes. In the dark he hastily takes off his shoes and clothes, leaving on only his underpants. Joyfully, he puts on the two-tone shoes. While he is lacing them, he realizes that someone is sobbing in the adjoining room. He gets up and, in underpants and shoes, goes into his bedroom. By the light of the lamp, he sees Esperanza, in bed, crying.

"Why are you crying?"

"Because you don't love me anymore."

Pereira shuts the door and walks toward his wife, saying vehemently:

"Yes, I do love you! Yes, I do love you!"

He takes hold of the sheet and, with a certain violence and a grandiose gesture, uncovers his wife. She is naked. He climbs on top of her with his shoes on.

"Yes, I do love you!" he tells her.

And she responds:

"Be careful, my liver hurts."

KILL THE LION!

# VII. A Day in the Country

M. Ripolin, purser on *La Navarra*, the French Transatlantic Line's ship that makes a stopover at Puerto Alegre, on its way from Cherbourg to New York, with a final destination of Buenos Aires, stands alongside the gangplank, manifest of cargo in hand, keeping watch over the unloading of two English ponies and twelve steamer trunks belonging to engineer Cussirat. Martín Garatuza, Spanish, short and squat, wearing a derby and black suit, with two hunting shotguns upon his shoulder, stands at his side.

Ripolin holds the receipt out to him.

"You're the owner of all this?" he asks in nasal Spanish.

"No, sir, but I am authorized to sign the receipt," says Garatuza, setting down a signature lavish with curlicues and then explaining: "I am señor Cussirat's valet. He arrives on the island tomorrow, in his airplane."

"In his airplane?" asks Ripolin, widening his eyes.

"He is a first-class pilot," Garatuza says proudly and breaks into a run down the gangplank, moving on short legs.

In order to return to Puerto Alegre, his native land, Pepe Cussirat left White Plains in his Blériot biplane, landed in Baltimore, slept in Charlotte, bought cigarettes in Atlanta, lunched in Tampa, spent fifteen days in Havana, waiting for a spare part, and spied the coast of Arepa at 10 A.M. on the 23$^{rd}$ of May 1926, a cloudless, unforgettable day in Arepan history.

The Ventosa Plain lies to the north of Puerto Alegre, three kilometers from the train station on the Paredón-Remedios line. The plain is a grassy green field, with a stream cutting through its middle and tamarind trees along the steam's banks; the plain is surrounded by three small hills named Cimarrón, Cerrito de Enmedio, and Destiladeros, on which cacao, coffee, and tobacco are sown.

By presidential order and with the object of making an easy landing for Cussirat's Blériot, the army has removed the pasturing cows, cut down a yucca that had grown in the center of the plain, and drawn a circle around the field to keep kids from starting to play there and being run over by the plane. The women from nearby huts have prepared fried fish and tamales to sell to the people who will be coming to see the landing.

That morning, for the first and last time in their history, the trains arrived at the Remedios station packed full. The director of the railroad company, Mr. Fisher, backed up the service with two coaches from the Guarapo-Chihualán line.

Pereira, in his pinstriped suit, borrowed straw boater, and two-toned shoes, arrived at Remedios on the 9:30 train and started walking, among poor families in their Sunday best and cruller vendors, along the dirt road leading to the Ventosa Plain.

After a while, Galvazo passed by, riding pillion on a police motorcycle, clinging to the back of the driver, with doña Rosita in the side-car, raising a cloud of dust and her arm to greet Pereira.

The Berriozábal's chauffeur, assisted by a servant, the gardener, and a maid, zealously watches over two baskets in the Dussemberg's trunk of Westphalian ham, roast turkey, and Gruyère cheese sandwiches, a jar of preserved nuts, three cans of Rodel *hors d'oeuvres*, a dozen oranges, six bottles of St. Emilión, three Thermoses of black coffee, a bottle of Martell, a chest of tableware, a collapsible table, and a tablecloth.

The Regalado sisters, dressed in blue and white with unfashionable flounces and Italian straw hats, have been seated in the back seat for half an hour.

Ángela, wearing a dress by Worth; don Carlitos, in a sport jacket and binoculars hanging on his sunken chest; Dr. Malagón, with an inappropriate broad-brimmed hat; Pepita Jiménez, languid; and doña Conchita Parmesano, brimming over with emotion, leave the house after having gone pee-pee, ready for the day in the country.

"And Tintín?" asks the stupider of the Regalado sisters.

"He went in the González Rolls," don Carlitos responds.

"Hello, my beauties," Malagón says to the Regalado sisters, putting a rheumatic foot up on the running board.

"At last, we're going to see an airplane!" says Conchita Parmesano.

"And Pepe Cussirat," says Ángela, "whom we haven't seen for fifteen years."

"Yes, if he doesn't crash on the way," says Pepita Jiménez, with a premonition of something terrible.

"God forbid! Knock on wood!" exclaims Conchita Parmesano.

"He'll get here all right, he'll love you just the same as before," Ángela assures the poetess, kissing and cuddling her.

Don Carlitos, a pain in the neck, counts the guests and tells each one where to sit, changing his mind several times and making them change places. The chauffeur whispers to Ángela:

"Everything fit in the trunk, señora."

Ángela, under her breath, tells Conchita:

KILL THE LION!

"We're bringing lovely snacks."

Conchita, with glutinous humor, rolls her eyes.

"It makes my mouth water just to think about the delicacies you must be taking."

"Will the ladies do me the favor of seating themselves in the back seat instead of gossiping?" Don Carlitos asks.

The ladies and Malagón squeeze into the rear of the car. Don Carlitos climbs in next to the driver, and the Dussemberg, its top down, takes off, requiring the ladies to hold onto their hats and burst into little shrieks.

The overland procession of paupers, growing denser, sweatier, dustier, and slower, parts from time to time in order to make way for the cars as they come by, honking rudely and raising clouds of dust. Alongside Pereira pass the presidential Studebaker with Cardona, green and solitary, inside; Bonilla, Paletón, and the Señor of the Network in a borrowed Mercedes; finally, the Berriozábals and company, without stopping, with friendly waves, obliging Pereira to doff his hat.

The Ventosa Plain is a desert at its center and a festival around the edges. Pereira walks amidst fried foods, crying children, bad-humored mothers, and spitting men, until he reaches the tamarind tree, reserved since last night, in whose shade the Berriozábals have established themselves with their car, their guests, and the small table of food.

"When we saw you," Ángela tells him, wiping away a spot of mayonnaise with a cambric handkerchief, "we were about to stop to ask you to come ride with us, but it was too late. You'd already gone a kilometer."

"But, woman! Ángela, what are you saying? Pereira needs the exercise," Malagón says, his mouth full of Westphalian ham.

"The suit fits you very well," Ángela says, eyeing Pereira up and down. She takes him by the arm and leads him to the table, where the chauffeur is doing the honors. "Have a snack. You must be hungry after your walk."

Bonilla, Paletón, and the Señor of the Network, who have joined the group, stand around the table, chewing. The chauffeur solemnly removes the damp cloth covering the sandwiches. Pereira looks at them, not knowing which to choose. A little runny-nosed Black boy, sticking a finger up his nose, watches the ceremony from a few meters away. Ángela sees him, is deeply moved, and, brimming with maternal and humane feelings, picks a sandwich from the stack and gives it to the boy, who studies it mistrustfully before biting it. Ángela returns to the others and excuses herself saying:

"I . . . things like that. . . I just can't stop myself."

They look at her sympathetically. Nobody sees that the boy bites into the sandwich, doesn't like it, and throws it on the ground.

Don Carlitos, standing up in the Dussemberg, his elbows leaning on the windshield bar while he looks through his binoculars, at that moment shouts:

"Here he comes! Here he comes!"

Without ceasing to chew, without setting down the sandwiches, everyone turns to look where the binoculars are pointing. In the sky there is a dot, growing in size.

# VIII. Cussirat's Airplane

The Blériot circles the plain, descends, bounces off the ground, lunges upward, accelerates, then begins ascending again; it circles once more and lands, bumping along, finally coming to a stop one meter from the arroyo, with a wing torn by the solitary acacia tree.

The spectators, observing the landing and overcome by admiration, recover and break the army's cordon, bursting into a run to view the flying machine up close.

Pepe Cussirat, wearing an aviator's cap and a silk scarf, his nose cold, gets to his feet in the cabin and then leaps to the ground. As he steps out of his coveralls, he sees how the wretchedly poor crowd is piling toward him. Children shouting, dogs barking, and everybody running toward the Blériot. Martín Garatuza, dressed in mechanic's work clothes, is the first to reach the plane. Cussirat, good-natured, doffs his cap and embraces him. Then the two of them bend over the wing to examine the tear. The people stop at a respectful distance; only a skinny mutt comes up, barking furiously. The Moderates, some of them older men, others young madcaps, as well as fellow carousers and Cussirat's childhood friends, make their way through the common people and approach to give him an affectionate hug.

"A sight for sore eyes!" don Carlitos says.

"Welcome to the Fatherland!" says Paletón.

"You made a phenomenal landing!" says young Paco Ridruejo, who has seen planes on his trip to Europe.

"Had a good trip?" asks don Bartolomé González, the owner of the Rolls.

"I had bad weather leaving Cuba," Cussirat says.

"Come have a bite to eat and a glass of wine," don Carlitos says, throwing his arm around Cussirat's shoulder. "You must be fainting with hunger."

"How is doña Ángela?" Cussirat asks.

"Dying to see you," don Carlitos responds.

Martín Garatuza comes up to Cussirat and reports respectfully:

"The tear is nothing, señor, it can be repaired in no time."

"Good," answers Cussirat, taking off his gloves and, turning to Berriozábal, adding: "Let's get going then."

Don Carlitos, delighted, turns to the people present and says:

"Come along, everyone, my wife has brought enough sandwiches for an army."

Cussirat, tall, good looking, tousled, distinguished, wearing a leather jacket with riding pants and boots, begins walking arm and arm with don Carlitos. The crowd makes way for him and looks at him respectfully, as at a priest of some new religion. The Moderates, old and young, follow along, gasping:

"How he's grown!"

"How he's changed!"

"How old he is!"

Behind the throng, at the end of the plain, in the shade of the tamarind tree, stand the women who have come to see Cussirat, saying:

"How handsome he is!"

"How tall!"

"How brave!"

Between Conchita Parmesano and the Regalado sisters, Pepita Jiménez trembles as she smoothes a wrinkle in her new dress and says nothing.

Ángela takes a few steps forward across the grass, clamping her hat down to avoid the warm breeze's sending it flying. Seeing her from afar, Cussirat detaches himself from don Carlitos and walks toward the group. Ángela, understanding that what is about to happen—namely, that Cussirat will greet her before anyone else—is impolite, turns her head and says:

"Come on, Pepita! What are you waiting for?"

Pepita, weak-kneed, insecure, feeling that her legs are not going to support her, stations herself alongside Ángela, as Cussirat, his arms spreading at three meters distance, exclaims:

"Ángela!"

Ángela realizes, horrified, that Cussirat has not recognized his former fiancée.

"Here's Pepita," she says.

Cussirat halts, disconcerted for a moment. He looks, unenchanted, into the huge eyes, filled with resentment, looking back at him; he looks at the white, sickly skin, the mouth, puckered now so as to appear smaller, but still half open, and says, self-controlled, feigning happiness:

"Pepita!"

He tries to embrace her, but she, blushing, twisting her neck, lowering her eyes, letting out a little nervous laugh that sounds more like a howl, prey to a moment of cowardice, holds out her hand, which Cussirat, once again disconcerted, shakes.

"How you've changed!" he says, to excuse his earlier confusion. "You're much more . . . pretty. More elegant."

Then, he turns to Ángela and hugs her affectionately.

Conchita Parmesano, the Regalado sisters, the Redondos, the Chabacanos, the daughters of don Remigio Iglesias and Fortunata Méndez, dressed in tulle, with parasols and broad-brimmed hats, moved, without quite knowing why, slightly jealous, observe from a few meters away.

A few meters farther back, solitary, with a sandwich in his hand, Pereira also observes how the recent arrival, slender, tall, dressed in who knows what, but well, greets, after Ángela, each of the ladies.

In the shade of the tamarind tree, the society girls, headed by the Regalado sisters, with their keepsake albums open against their breasts, form a line so that Cussirat, leaning on the Dussemberg's trunk alongside Ángela, may set down a remembrance and an autograph for them.

The men, around the table, eat, drink, and talk about mechanics.

Farther away, Pepita Jiménez, armed with a net, is trying to catch a butterfly.

And still farther away, from the back of the presidential Studebaker, Cardona solicitously tells don Carlitos, who is beside him:

"The Marshal wants to see him. I don't dare speak to him, because I don't know him, but you tell him to come to the palace tonight, at nine."

Don Carlitos, delighted with the mission, fearful of not being able to carry it out, and wanting to make himself important, says:

"I'll see what can be done, señor Cardona, you can count on my best efforts. I'll try to bring him myself."

"I've come to say good-bye, señora," Pereira says, with the boater in his hand, to Ángela, who has one foot up on the Dussemberg's running board.

"Pepe," Ángela addresses Cussirat, who is at her side, "I'd like to present señor Pereira, a great draftsman and an inspired violinist."

Pereira, full of admiration, and Cussirat, distracted, exchange the required "glad to meet you."

"We can't take you," Ángela explains to Pereira, "because there are already so many of us."

"Don't give it a thought, señora," says Pereira, "I'm used to walking."

Ángela, forgetting about Pereira and looking all around, asks:

"Where's my husband?"

Don Carlitos, happy, comes bounding up to his car.

"Let's not hear anything about your coming behind us," he says to Cussirat, "you're coming along with me, get in, because I've got to give you a fabulous message."

Cussirat obeys, half-heartedly, says good-bye to Pereira, smiling slightly and minimally polite, then walks around the car to get in between don Carlitos and the chauffeur. To the sound of slamming doors and the cries of its occupants, the Dussemberg takes off, crammed full. Ángela, busy extricating a sunshade caught between Malagón's legs and the poetess's petticoats, neither bids farewell nor looks at Pereira, who remains behind, putting on his hat, watching them leave, more satisfied than resentful.

Later, Pereira heaves a realistic sigh and begins to walk among the people. The mothers, disheveled, sweating, ill-humored, carrying pissy babies in their arms, shout like generals trying to round up their troops for a retreat; the men drain the dregs

KILL THE LION!

of *aguardiente* right from the bottle; the last cars leave the plain, bumping along. Pereira stops and turns his eyes toward the Blériot, which sits, solitary in the middle of the plain. Martín Garatuza, with a piece of burlap, is wiping off the oil drips with all the affection of a groom rubbing down a sweating thoroughbred.

# ix. A Passing Temptation

"I hope you understand, Pepe, what this means," don Carlitos says to Cussirat, before arriving at the palace. "For us both. For you and for me."

He adjusts his tiepin. Cussirat does not respond. Through the window of the Dion-Button he keeps looking at the badly lit streets, the scrawny dogs, the endless puddles. Looking at them and recognizing them.

"It's an honor to be the Moderate Party's candidate," don Carlitos presses on, "I don't deny it. But if the Marshal sends for you, it's not in order to say hello. I assure you, he's going to toss you a big fat proposition. He wants to buy you. And in these cases, Pepe, listen to the voice of experience, the voice of a man who has suffered a lot, and who's telling you: a bird in the hand's worth a hundred in the bush. Unless there's a miracle, you've lost the election. On the other hand, if you accept the Marshal's proposition, whatever it is, you come out a winner, and I come out winning too, for having delivered you. It's a favor I'm doing the Marshal and its one I'll endeavor to make sure he doesn't forget. If you don't accept the proposition, whatever it is, you'll be left adrift, the candidate of a dying party, and I'll be left in a bad way."

"How left in a bad way, don Carlitos? You did your part by delivering me."

"Because that's politics, my boy. I'm your godfather, and I'm responsible for what you do."

The palace stairs are marble, in imitation of some ancient Venetian palace. Don Carlitos and Cussirat, in dark suits, stiff collars, with hats in hand, climb up, led by an attendant.

"Now you'll see," don Carlitos says, "he's very good-natured."

Cussirat, instead of answering, yawns, putting one hand over his mouth. Belaunzarán's voice disconcerts him, causing him to stumble:

"Welcome!"

Belaunzarán stands at the top of the stairs, smiling, clutching the lapels of an impeccable gray suit, which gives his body the shape of a torpedo. Don Carlitos, triumphant, gives a hop and a little cry before making the introduction.

"Marshal, sir, it is an honor to bring you this rotten kid. Engineer Cussirat, the President of the Republic, don Manuel Belaunzarán."

Belaunzarán shakes Cussirat's hand with the straightforwardness typical of men in high office. Cussirat responds in the same way, because he knows that while Belaunzarán may wear epaulettes, he was born on a straw mat.

"We've heard about each other," Belaunzarán explains to don Carlitos, smiling at Cussirat, so as to make him aware that they are both celebrities.

"Pleased to meet you," says Cussirat.

Don Carlitos, who wants to emphasize the magnificence of the introduction he has just performed, exclaims:

"You two make me feel like a poor devil!"

Belaunzarán looks at don Carlitos condescendingly, mentally agreeing with him, and, raising his hand in the direction of a corridor, says to his visitors:

"Come this way."

The usher understands that his services are no longer needed. As the three other men move down the corridor, between *fin-de-siècle* bronzes, he descends the stairs, reaches his little hole in the wall, seats himself before his table, and instantly falls asleep.

The president and his visitors are seated in the despot's private office; Belaunzarán in a high-backed chair, in which his belly does not get in the way of his legs; don Carlitos and Cussirat at opposite ends of a short, Moroccan-leather sofa. Belaunzarán recites a short prepared speech that omits any mention of Cussirat's candidacy, instead dealing with the importance of aviation's coming to Arepa.

"This event paves the way for progress," he says.

As Belaunzarán speaks, don Carlitos pays dim-witted attention while Cussirat absent-mindedly looks around the room. By the light of a lamp from which dangle strings of beads, he observes the large desk, suitable for a mental Pantagruel but on which only edicts, evil laws, and death sentences have been signed; a portrait of the master, with the national flag across his chest, hanging on the wall; a bust of the same figure on a shelf, nude, Herculean, restored to youth, in Italian marble.

Belaunzarán goes on with his story and comes to the point:

"The time has come to undertake the creation of an Arepan air force."

Cussirat's eyes cease wandering and are fix on the speaker. Don Carlitos straightens up, his heart paralyzed, his eyes shining.

Seeing that the bull is set up, Belaunzarán turns in profile to give the final thrust:

"I want you to take charge of everything," he tells Cussirat. "I name you commander-in-chief of the air force, with the rank of aerial vice-admiral. You'll go to Europe, at government expense, and buy six pursuit planes, whichever seem the best to you."

Don Carlitos cannot contain himself and says:

"Pepe, I told you it was worthwhile coming here!"

Belaunzarán rises to his feet, crosses his hands behind his back, takes a few steps, stops, turns to Cussirat, and asks him:

"What do you think?"

Cussirat is puzzled:

"What is the object?"

"Of creating an air force?" Belaunzarán shifts his posture, extends his arms, and then crosses them over his chest, in order to explain the obvious:

"Engineer, your trip will demonstrate not only that the airplane can reach Arepa but that Arepa can reach many places by airplane. With a squadron we would be in the position to defend our territorial rights."

"You're referring to Huanábana Island?" asks Cussirat.

"And Corunga," Belaunzarán replies.

"And the Golondrinas Islands!" adds don Carlitos, "which in the time of the Spanish were ruled by the Regency of Santa Cruz de Arepa."

Cussirat does not respond immediately, leaving open the possibility that Belaunzarán's reasoning seems foolish to him.

"But an air force," he says, finally, "costs a lot of money. Wouldn't it be an economic disaster for the country?"

"It's all figured out," Belaunzarán says. "Creating an air force is cheaper than buying a naval cruiser, and it's more impressive. On the other hand, it's a matter of prestige, which sooner or later will redound to our benefit."

Cussirat, pensive, buries himself in the Moroccan leather;

Belaunzarán lights up a cigar; don Carlitos is beside himself with joy:

"What great news!" he says.

And Belaunzarán:

"On your trip to Europe, Engineer, you will hire six pilots yourself."

"Two would be enough," Cussirat advises. "They could help me train Arepan pilots."

Belaunzarán, who is on his way to the bathroom, stops short.

"Never!" He opens the bathroom door, cigar in his mouth, as he unbuttons the top button of his fly, and mutters between his teeth:

"In case of a revolution, I don't want six numbskulls coming to bomb my house."

Ending the sentence, he closes the door. Don Carlitos and Cussirat are left alone.

"What an opportunity, my boy!" says don Carlitos. "Don't waste it!"

"But I really came here for something else! I came to be a presidential candidate!"

"What presidential candidate—in a pig's eye! Don't be frivolous! Think! Commander-in-chief! Aerial vice-admiral! You're going to be the most important man in Arepa!"

The sound of flushing water from the bathroom drowns his enthusiasm, and obliges him to keep quiet and think about something else. The door opens. Belaunzarán returns, buttoning his fly and asking:

"Well then, what do you have to say? You accept?"

Cussirat, smoking an English Oval, inhales before answering. Don Carlitos, impatient, answers for him:

"Of course he accepts!"

KILL THE LION!

Cussirat exhales the smoke idly:

"I need time to think about it."

"How much time? Twenty minutes? Thirty?" Belaunzarán hounds him, energetically.

"Two days," says Cussirat.

Belaunzarán makes an impatient face but quickly resigns himself.

"All right, I grant you two days. Come see me here, the day after tomorrow at the same time."

Cussirat and don Carlitos descend the empty staircase. Don Carlitos, annoyingly, prods Cussirat:

"Say yes, Pepe. Say yes, say you're going to say yes to him."

Cussirat stops for a moment on the stairs, looks, in a kindly way, into the other man's expectant eyes, smiles sadly, and says:

"I'm going to say…"

The elegant beauty and distinction of his face cracks for a moment as he inserts his tongue between his lips and teeth and makes the sound of a monumental fart, moving at the same time, with a skill no one would have suspected, both his arms and his hands in a coarse gesture. Don Carlitos's spirits pass from outrage to prostration. His chest caves in, his shoulders droop, he lowers his eyes, his eyebrows rise aslant, his mouth hangs half open. Cussirat regains his composure and continues down the stairs.

"Let's go to the casino," he says.

The old boy follows him, crestfallen. And he would follow still more crestfallen if he knew that from the balcony railing, between cherubs and shadow, Belaunzarán, who has seen it all, is studying them while clenching his jaws and raising an eyebrow. When they get out of sight, he turns half way around and begins pacing, pensive, his hands crossed behind his back, down the dark corridor. What starts out as a philosophic stroll turns into a furious charge when Belaunzarán fully realizes the insult to which he has been subjected.

Going past the Hall of Treaties, the Chinese Hall, his private office, and the Green Room, he stops in front of the last door in the corridor and pulls it open violently.

From the armchair where he has been reading *El Mundo* and dozing, Cardona raises his eyes and trembles. Belaunzarán enters, like a crazed elephant, slamming the door behind him.

"The jig's up! There will be no air force! There's no dealing with that fop! I proposed naming him aerial vice-admiral, and he comes back with he needs time to think it over—two days! I grant him the time, and a couple of minutes later, when he's going downstairs, he tells the pimp who brought him here that he's going to answer me ... *plplptt!*" He lays a fake fart and wrings his hands in exact imitation of Cussirat's gesture.

Cardona blushes. Belaunzarán goes on:

"If *plplptt* is his answer, I'm going to give him a *plplptt!*"

# x. Living it up and Afterward

They are living it up at the casino. In the members dinning hall, a dinner has been prepared and consumed to celebrate the return of Pepe Cussirat. A white tablecloth has been laid on the round table with place settings for twelve. They have eaten, they have drunk, and they have stained the tablecloth with squid ink, sauce from the chicken a la galopina and *mousse au chocolat*. Andrés Arrechederre, Spanish born, narrow-minded, and risen to *maître d'hôtel* at the Puerto Alegre Casino, picks up empty bottles of Chablis and Valpolicella, assisted by Peabrain Pablito, who carries out, on a tray, the remains of the blow-out so as to leave the men to the intimacy of coffee, Cuban cigars, Martell, and Malagón's chatter.

"When King Narizotas got married, it was nothing to write home about: a bomb on the Gran Vía, a bomb on San Antonio, a bomb in the sacristy. We didn't kill him, but he must have had a phenomenal wedding night."

Pepe Cussirat, Coco Regalado, Paco Ridruejo, and Horse González, childhood friends and the latest litter of good-for-nothings, add their belly laughs to those of their predecessors: don Miguel Barrientos, his leg much better; don Bartolomé González, Horse's father; and don Casimiro Paletón, who has set aside the black suit and dressed himself like a bohemian. Don Carlitos smiles half-heartedly because, with his liver, the dinner has gone down badly. Bonilla and the Señor of the Network, who are models of civic responsibility, pull disapproving faces. Don Ignacio Redondo, who was a monarchist in his youth, before coming to Arepa, and now is timorous, says to Malagón:

"And for the one bad night you gave the king, you and your bones ended up in Arepa?"

Malagón rises to his feet and, looking at the crystal chandelier, declaims:

"Blessed land, in which I was not born."

A belly laugh and patriotic applause.

"Was it worth it?" Redondo asks.

The young men's jaws drop, and they pretend to be offended by the question's implied insult to their country. Malagón replies that he considers it a privilege to have come to this country, and Redondo, beating a retreat, concludes by swearing that he feels himself "as much an Arepan as the next person."

Bonilla and the Señor of the Network get to their feet in order to say goodnight.

"It's time to go home to bed," explains Bonilla, who drinks not a drop, when someone urges them to stay. Approaching Cussirat, he says:

"Tomorrow, calmly, we'll talk about your campaign, Engineer."

Don Carlitos, turned green, says:

"I'm leaving with you two."

Redondo, who does not want to commit another *faux pas* and who feels his presence superfluous, also leaves.

Without the long faces, the party livens up.

"Bring on the whores!" pleads Coco Regalado.

"Yes, bring them on!" several others chime in, applauding.

"If they do," warns don Bartolomé Caballo, "sh-h-h, not a

word to your mother, or you're no longer a member of the casino."

Another outburst of laughter.

"Don't worry, father," says Horse, who has appeared in *Don Juan Tenorio*, "my lips are sealed."

Pepe Cussirat takes the initiative and calls on Andresillo, the solicitor general, telling him to order up some whores from doña Faustina's.

"Bring on the Princess," commands Paletón, a connoisseur, "to dance the *jota*."

"And a mulatta for me," Cussirat requests.

And that night the Princess came, with seven girls, in a hired horse cart, and danced the *jota* with Cussirat. When, tapping her feet, she turned over the table and broke the glasses, Pepe said to Ridruejo, helping him up from the floor:

"Like in the good old days!"

Afterward, he threw himself on top of a consumptive Black girl.

So the night passed, and daylight found them wildly euphoric, blanket tossing Peabrain Pablito in the casino patio.

At noon on a stifling day, the next after his arrival, Pepe Cussirat opens his eyes in his room and does not recognize it. His dull gaze wanders over the walls hung with tapestries, the huge wardrobe, the marble-topped dressing table, the pitcher and washbasin; he halts his gaze, puzzled, at the photograph of his grandfather, dressed as a student, clutching a mandolin; finally, he lifts his eyes to the blinds, where the light, the suffocating mid-day heat, and the lazy creaking of a wagon, passing by on calle Cordobanes, filter in. That is when he understands that he is in Puerto Alegre. He recognizes as well that the tinkling he hears comes from the bubbles of Sal

Hepática that Martín Garatuza is stirring in a glass on the night table.

"It's noon, señor."

Cussirat raises himself up. He has a pasty mouth, fetid breath, parched throat, sore muscles, and in the depths of his being, forebodings, misgivings. He drinks the Sal Hepática. Garatuza opens the blinds.

"A filet with potatoes, señor?"

Cussirat gestures in disgust.

"Do you want your at-home clothes, or should I get ready what you're going to wear this afternoon, to go to the Berrio-zábal's house?"

Cussirat wants to go back to sleep, gestures with his hand for Garatuza to leave, a gesture Garatuza ignores.

"Don Francisco Ridruejo is in the drawing room, waiting for you, señor."

Cussirat sits up in bed, ill tempered.

A few minutes later, Paco Ridruejo comes into the room, wearing peasant garb.

"On your feet, lazy bones," he orders, "today's May 24th."

"So?"

"You still don't remember? It's the anniversary of capturing the Pedernal. I want you to see your opponent in action."

Cussirat, brushing aside his fatigue, his hangover from the binge, and his bad mood, gets to his feet.

# XI. Capturing the Pedernal

At the end of the sixteenth century, the Spanish decided to build a fort to defend Puerto Alegre from pirates. For erecting the fort, they chose the small island of Pedernal (named for the flint somebody found there), which lies at the mouth of the bay.

Fort Pedernal, which served the purpose of keeping hostile ships from entering (or leaving) the port, was never good for anything, because pirates never reached Santa Cruz de Arepa. The men who built it never could have imagined that the fortifications they were building would, with the passing of time, turn into the trap into which a Spanish army would fall, when General Santander and the remains of his reduced forces sought refuge there after the Battle of Rebenco.

The Spanish resisted for eleven months in that last redoubt. In truth, it was not hard for them, because nobody attacked them during that time, nor did they resist because they wanted to, but because nobody came after them. The garrison had been forgotten by the civilized world, as a deputy to Cortés put it, when news of the massacre became known.

After eleven months on the site (relatively speaking, because the Spanish traveled every afternoon to the mainland in order to put in supplies), Belaunzarán, the youngest of the insurgent leaders, decided to strike a blow that would forever put an end to the Spanish domination of Arepa. On the beach, he gathered the Blacks from Humareda and the Guarupa Indians from Paso de Cabras, and when it grew dark and the tide was lower, he stripped off his colorful brigadier general's uniform and, in his birthday suit, with only a machete in his hand, waded into water up to his waist, turned to face the Blacks and Guarupas, who were watching him without understanding what was afoot, and, raising the machete, shouted:

"I go after glory! Whoever seeks glory, follow me!"

This said, he placed the machete between his teeth and started swimming toward the island. One thousand men followed him, swimming naked, biting down on machetes. Many of them drowned, but many also crossed the one-hundred-meter-wide channel separating the island from the mainland, and they fell like a lightning bolt upon the 143 Spaniards, who were taken by surprise, holding a celebration in honor of Mary, Mother of Mercy, and commemorating the marvelous victory of the Spanish ships at Lepanto. It was the 24th of May. Not one Spaniard was left alive.

Don Casimiro Paletón, who was a bad young poet at that time, sang this battle in a poem of a thousand sonorous lines (one for each of the participants) in which he described Belaunzarán, who was then twenty-four years old, as the Boy Hero—for which he had never sufficiently repented.

Each year on May 24th, the Blacks from Humareda and the Indians from Paso de Cabras assemble on the beach and dance for six hours to the sound of bongo drums before the diplomatic corps, the functionaries, and the port's riffraff. At six, Belaunzarán, on horseback, dressed as a brigadier general, arrives. He takes off the uniform, remains in his shorts, puts a machete between his teeth, and repeats the act of swimming to

Pedernal, where there awaits him, with music, the Artillery Band and a young lady, dressed as the Fatherland, who crowns him with laurels.

Many men follow him across the channel and, every year, someone drowns. The proverbial hope of the Arepa's rich is "that El Gordo drowns swimming to Pedernal." A wish never fulfilled in the twenty-eight years that have passed since Independence.

Pepe Cussirat and Paco Ridruejo lunched at the English Hotel and arrived at the beach dressed in white, with Panamas on their heads, and at 4:30, when the dancing was reaching its height.

Under an arbor, seated on a wicker chair, Sir John Phipps sleeps peacefully, thanks to his deafness. Beside him, the first secretary of the British Embassy, is shooing the flies.

Clearing a path among the remains of fried fish and green coconut shells that cover the sand, the two young dandies reach the Ticket Arbor, greeting along the way Bonilla, Paletón, and the Señor of the Network, who are yawning in the Deputies Arbor. While Paco Ridruejo pays for the chairs, someone on the balcony cordially greets Cussirat. He returns the greeting and, when his companion sits down at his side, asks him:

"Who's that?"

Ridruejo looks over at the man, who, seated on a long bench, doffs his boater for the second time, nods his head, and smiles.

"He's a musician, a protégé of Ángela Berriozábal."

Cussirat does not recall Pereira, who, accompanied by his wife, his mother-in-law, and doña Rosita Galvazo, is enjoying the spectacle for free, because Galvazo, who is in charge of security, has given them passes.

The Guarupas dance to the sound of kettledrums, bells, reed flutes, and big guitars; the Blacks to the beat of bongos and African *tumba* drums. All at the same time, without coordination. Everybody gets drunk, some fight, others fall down on the sand, prostrate with exhaustion, and there they lie, sleeping off a hangover.

The Artillery Band and the school children reach Pedernal in installments, on the harbormaster's launch. Don Carlitos and don Ignacio Redondo, afraid their absence might be noticed and result in countless irreparable injuries, turn up in a bad mood at the last minute. Coco Regalado and Horse González, in the revelers' wake, show up drunk, stumbling around "to see how El Gordo drowns."

Finally Belaunzarán arrives, in the midst of the mob's clamor and the uproar of the warring bands. He disrobes, wades into the sea, says his celebrated phrase, and crosses the channel without mishap, at the head of hundreds of drunks.

When he appears on the other shore and is crowned by the Fatherland, to the sound of the Arepan anthem and the flare of fireworks, Cussirat, between rounds of applause, the bongos, and the din, standing on a chair in order to see better, turns to Paco Ridruejo and says:

"Nobody can fight against this man in an election. He must be killed."

A moment goes by before the other man convinces himself that his friend is talking in earnest. Then, he says:

"Yes, of course! But how?"

That night at the casino, the Moderates got the surprise and some of them the conniption of their lives. Pepe Cussirat, their last hope, rejected the candidacy for president.

"But you sent a cable saying that you accepted the candidacy," Bonilla complains bitterly.

"That I accepted it 'in principle,'" Cussirat corrects him. "Now I refuse it. I have thought it over, and I have seen the reality. In the first place, I don't think I have a chance of being elected; and second, I think that, even were some sort of a miracle to happen and we were to win the election, Belaunzarán, who obviously doesn't want to give up his power, as the death of Dr. Saldaña and the revisions that have been made to the Constitution show, has the necessary strength and the popularity to start a revolution and snatch the presidency from us in two days. Then we would really be in a tight spot. Me, and you people."

His argument, which would seem incontrovertible, and may be formulated in a single question: "Why fight when there's no hope?" did not convince either the stubbornest Moderates, or the more moderate, such as Bonilla, Paletón, and the Señor of the Network, who have been talking for fifteen years of waging civic battles, or the most timid, such as don Ignacio Redondo, to whom the specter of the Law of Expropriation gives sleepless nights. The rest, such as don Carlitos, don Bartolomé González, and Barrientos, who believe that if you can't win, you have to remain, at the very least, on good terms with the man who does, understand Cussirat, excuse him, and even defend him when he gets up, leaves the auditorium, and goes to have a Tom Collins at the casino bar; but they lose the battle when don Carlitos proposes Belaunzarán as the Moderate Party's candidate for president, because the reactionary, intransigent, and Obscurantist forces, as Belaunzarán would call them, outnumber them.

"We can't put ourselves in his hands and let him lop off our heads," says Redondo, not thinking about his own neck, but about his income from the department store bearing his name.

After a lot of debating, and with the creation of ill will, they agree on speaking with Belaunzarán and asking that the elections be postponed, with the aim of gaining more time for deciding which candidate to name.

# XII. Tête-à-tête and Antechamber

The peacock throws back its head, raises the feathers on its craw, lifts its tail, leaving its anus exposed, fans out the tail, and screams. Two thrushes fly away, another peacock answers, a crow turns its head and looks sideways, mistrustfully. A chained macaw perches on its ring, its tongue chiming in.

Ángela and Cussirat are walking along the garden path, taking in the 5 o'clock coolness.

"I would like to do something," says Ángela, "but I don't know what. I need someone to advise me."

"When I first got here," Cussirat says, "I had hopes of being able to win the election, and of Belaunzarán's not being totally malign. After yesterday's interview and the Pedernal ceremony, those hopes went up in smoke. The election is lost, and this man is going to lead the country into disaster. An end must be put to him. By any means whatsoever."

Ángela, alert, stops and, looking at a wild lime plant, asks, "By what means?"

Cussirat lets her turn her back to him and put her nose into the flowers before responding. Looking at his hostess's buttocks, and putting his hands into the pockets of his impeccable trousers, he says:

"By killing him."

Ángela, alert, smelling the flowers, without turning her face, with her heart pounding, asks:

"Who is going to kill him?"

Cussirat, tense, lets a moment go by before answering:

"Ángela, I have to confess something to you."

Ángela turns around and looks at him, straight on.

"But, in the name of our friendship," Cussirat says, "I beg you, even though what I'm going to tell you sounds crazy, not to repeat it to anyone."

Ángela, deep voiced, filled with an irrelevant sensuality, says:

"Tell me!"

"The horses that I ordered to be sent here, the golf clubs, the shotguns, the twelve trunks of equipment—they're all nothing more than a smoke screen. Actually, if everything goes right, I'm thinking about leaving Arepa tonight."

Ángela experiences a tremble, half sincere and half feigned. In an elegant gesture, passionate and suggestive, she touches the sleeve of Cussirat's jacket, at the same time that she says, in a faltering voice:

"So soon?"

Cussirat, moving quickly, catches Ángela's hand and presses it against the worsted of his jacket.

"My mission will be accomplished."

Ángela looks at him, not understanding, or pretending not to understand. Cussirat frees Ángela's hand, turns 45° and remains absorbed in the flight of a bee. Ángela's hand grasps his arm, squeezes it lightly, and, with great skill, obliges it to brush against her breast.

"Tell me more," she pleads.

Cussirat, pompous, serious, imbued with the grandness of his intentions, tells her:

"For a month now, ever since I read in the newspapers about the assassination of Dr. Saldaña and received the Moderate's invitation, I've understood that I still owe a debt to my country: to free it from the tyrant. No matter how. I came for that. I come prepared."

"How brave you are!" Ángela says.

Cussirat lowers his eyes, silently conceding the truth of what she says. She asks him:

"Are you taking risks?"

"What's necessary. Tonight he'll receive me. I'll shoot him dead in his office. I'll try to get out of the palace alive. I've secured a car. My valet will be waiting for me in it, and he'll take me to Ventosa. The plane's ready. We'll both go away."

Ángela looks at him, full of admiration.

"Is there nothing I can do?"

"Nothing, for the moment. If something turns out badly, I'll tell you."

"Count on me."

Both continue walking down the path, slowly, immersed in their mutual admiration and their complicity.

Suddenly, Ángela stops, lets go of Cussirat's arm, and stoops down to pick from the ground a butterfly, which, having just emerged from its pupa, cannot fly and is stumbling clumsily on the path. She lifts it up and says to it:

"Get off the walk, somebody may step on you."

She places the butterfly on an acanthus leaf, while Cussirat watches her, moved. Then, together, they continue on their way.

The butterfly, on the acanthus, takes a few steps, slips, and falls onto the pathway.

The cathedral clock strikes 9 P.M. Cussirat's car, a Citroën, with Garatuza at the wheel, enters the Plaza Mayor, skirts some loose paving stones, and stops in front of the main door of the palace. The headlights go out, Garatuza gets out of the car, pounds the doorknocker against the door. Meanwhile, Cussirat checks his pistol for the last time and puts it in the holster he wears in his armpit.

"Engineer Cussirat would like to see el señor Presidente," Garatuza says to the porter who opens the door. The porter gives the message to his boss, who transmits it to the watch officer, who, in turn, transmits it to the second usher, who comes to the door and says to Garatuza:

"Come in."

Garatuza goes back to the car, opens the door, Cussirat gets out, enters the palace, and, led by the second usher, crosses the vestibule, the main patio, and, through the corridor of the mirrors, reaches the Venetian staircase, ascends, and on the second floor, to the right, enters the high, long, narrow, and dimly lit waiting room, its walls adorned with oil paintings of heroes of the Independence who passed on to the tomb's glory without attaining power. Along three walls stand soporific and abandoned chairs, and at the back, turned away from the fourth wall, sits the first usher before his desk.

"Kindly be seated," the second usher says to Cussirat.

Slightly impatient, Cussirat sits down. The second usher crosses the chamber, going over to where the first usher is seated, and speaks with him privately. The first usher, in talking, makes a series of gestures that may be interpreted in several ways. Finally, he addresses Cussirat, who is at the other end of the chamber, and says:

"What do you want?"

Cussirat rises to his feet and crosses the chamber.

"I'm Cussirat," he says, coming up in front of the desk.

It is of no use. The first usher looks at him uncomprehendingly, the second reprovingly.

"How may I help you?" asks the first usher.

Impatient, Cussirat takes out his card and hands it to him. "El señor Presidente is expecting me."

The first usher studies the card, the second withdraws. The first usher pushes a pad of paper toward Cussirat, and says:

"Write down your name and the business that brings you here."

"My name is on the card and, as for the business, el señor Presidente already knows about it. Give him my card."

"I'm sorry but this is the formality that must be gone through by everyone who speaks with el señor Presidente."

"I spoke with him the day before yesterday, and I went through no formality."

The usher is not perturbed.

"There must have been orders to the contrary. Now there are none," he offers Cussirat a pen. "If you'll be so good as to ..."

Livid, Cussirat writes in violent strokes: "Cussirat" "Air Force." He tears off the sheet and hands it to the usher, who rises and says:

"Be seated, I will convey your message."

With that, he leaves the room. Cussirat, furious, instead of sitting down walks from one side of the room to the other; then, still more furious and feeling himself ridiculous, he sits down.

Amid the smoke and the stench of the Havana cigars, the guffaws of his friends, and the clicking of the dominoes, Belaunzarán reads Cussirat's slip of paper. The usher, paralyzed with respect and toadying, bends at his side, awaiting the words that will come from his mouth. Cardona, Borunda, the majority leader, and Chucho Sardanápolo, minister of Public Welfare, seated in the chairs that the empress of China sent as a gift to King Cristóbal of Haiti but that arrived in Arepa by mistake, shuffle the dominoes, telling stories.

"Tell him I agree," says Belaunzarán, "he should wait for me."

The usher withdraws, bowing. The loud laughing immediately dies down. Sardanápolo says to Belaunzarán:

"Did you hear the joke about the nun who didn't want bread and cheese?"

Belaunzarán takes a puff on his cigar as the bootlickers grow silent, waiting for his answer.

"No, I heard a better one. About the young gentleman who didn't know whether to be vice-admiral or president."

"Tell it!" begs Borunda, eager to hear a joke from Belaunzarán's own mouth, so he can repeat it later, boasting: "Manuel himself told me this."

"It's a secret," Belaunzarán says, and takes another puff on his cigar.

The others look at him in silence, without knowing if they have committed a *faux pas*.

Ten o'clock and eleven o'clock find Cussirat seated in the antechamber, looking at the nodding, dozing usher. Ten o'clock and eleven o'clock find Garatuza sitting anxiously in the car. At 11:30, in the hallway, the commotion resounds of the group leaving, of the men going downstairs, laughing heartily at what the boss is saying, of the doors that open and close, and of the cars starting up in the back patio.

Cussirat's impatience has disappeared, or, better put, turned into a contained rage that is going to have consequences. Indifferent, without protest, he listens to the men leaving. He sees how the usher wakes up, gives a start, settles down, yawns, gets up, goes out of the room, stretching, and returns, after a little while, trying to look serious and with a message:

"El señor presidente had to go out on an urgent matter. He left word for you to come tomorrow, at noon."

Cussirat stands up, throws the cigarette he is smoking into a spittoon, glances at the usher, picks up his hat, and clears out.

# XIII. The Day they Dynamited the Palace

The first thing Cussirat does on arriving home is telephone Ángela. Fearful that the operator may overhear them, they make their conversation brief:

"I failed," he says.

"I'm glad," she says.

Cussirat hangs up.

Most of the night he stays awake. With Garatuza's help he assembles the bomb. He takes the explosives out of the golf bag, the detonator from the first-aid kit, the magnesium from the hatbox, one of the heads from inside the camera, and another from a wind-up alarm clock.

With a surgeon's skill, on the dining room table, using the parts Garatuza passes to him, he assembles the bomb and fits it inside a Thermos.

It is a simple bomb that can function in two ways, as the need may be. One by means of a clockwork mechanism, the other with a pressure device. In the first instance, the head is an alarm clock, whose hammer hits the detonator capsule and breaks it at the appointed time. The substance inside the capsule reacts with the magnesium surrounding it, thus producing a small explosion that serves to set off the dynamite at the bottom of the Thermos. In the second instance, the head is a coil mechanism that ends in a point. Upon pressing the head, the mechanism is compressed, the point pierces the capsule, and the effect described is produced.

At 4:00 A.M., having assembled the bomb and tested it, Cussirat puts it, along with the two heads, in a briefcase, locks it, yawns, and, leaving Garatuza to finish up, goes off to his bedroom, where silk pajamas with many frog fasteners await him, spread across the bed.

Coronel Epigmenio Pantoja's widow, who has come to collect overdue payments on his pension; a Protestant pastor; a seller of Spanish olives; and a persistent creditor are waiting, along with Cussirat, for an audience in the reception room.

Cussirat, elegant and nervous, with a pistol in his armpit and the briefcase full of dynamite, chain-smokes English Ovals. The usher treks back and forth, promises, and nobody gets in.

"El señor presidente will receive the lady who came first in one minute."

It is 1:30.

At that moment, like three vultures, dressed in black, solemn, filled with unjustified hopes, the Moderates, Bonilla, Paletón, and the Señor of the Network, enter the chamber. Seeing Cussirat, they give a start. Then they collect themselves. They cross the room looking straight ahead, noses up in the air, as though navigating through fetid air, and reach the usher to whom they say:

"We are from the Moderate Party. We wish to see the president of the Republic."

The attendant jumps, blushes, smiles, sweats, and says:

"Please go in."

And the four of them exit together, going toward the private office without paying any attention to the widow, who says: "Wasn't he going to receive me?" or to the creditor's curse, or to the Protestant minister's blush, or to the patience of the olive salesman, or to Cussirat, who has stood up and, briefcase in hand, is following after them.

In the hall, facing the door into the private office, the Señor of the Network says to Bonilla:

"Go on in, sir."

"Certainly not," responds the gentleman, "allow our friend Paletón, who has greater facility with words."

Paletón is startled:

"But what are you saying, sir? You are the one with the golden tongue. After you, as always."

"The majority agrees, sir," says the Señor of the Network, playing at parliamentary procedure, "go on in."

Bonilla has no alternative but to go in first. He puffs out his chest and says:

"All right, gentlemen, so be it."

He closes his fleshy mouth, which he wishes were smaller, with a bitter expression and, gloomier than ever, goes into Belaunzarán's office as onto a battlefield.

Without getting up before greeting them from his desk, Belaunzarán indicates to the attendant where he is to put the chairs on which the recent arrivals are to be seated.

After a brief hesitation, the Señor of the Network and Paletón decide who must go first, enter, and shut the door.

In the deserted hallway, Cussirat, as though walking by, one hand in the bag and his hat and briefcase in the other, passes in front of the door to the private office, which filters the mingled voices from inside; he comes to the next door, stops, grasps the handle, discreetly looks right and left. No one sees him. He moves his hand. The doorknob turns and the door yields. He opens it halfway, sees that there is no one inside, sees that there is no one outside, takes a step, and is in the Green Room.

He studies the tapestries and the Imperial style furniture in search of a good place for hiding the bomb. He decides on a marble-topped console. He puts the briefcase on top, opens it and takes out the Thermos and clockwork head. He consults his vest-pocket watch: it is 1:30. He sets the alarm for 2 o'clock in the afternoon, winds the clock, and is screwing in the head when he realizes that there is another door at the end of the room. Leaving the Thermos and bomb head on the console, he goes toward this recently discovered door, glues his ear to it, does not hear a sound, opens it, and is left pleasantly surprised. In the midst of marble, white tiles, presidential towels, is Marshal Belaunzarán's English bathroom.

The euphoria of this discovery lasts a second. Then he sets to work. At one leap he returns to the console, picks up the Thermos, changes the head, also changing the clockwork for the pressure device. He puts the first in his briefcase, goes into the bathroom, lowers the toilet lid, stands on it, sinks the Thermos into the water tank, placing it directly under the lever connected to the chain, gets down from the toilet, leaves the bathroom, and closes the door. In the Green Room, he picks up his hat and briefcase, goes to the door that opens onto the hallway, half opens it, sees that the hall is empty, and heaves a sigh of relief.

He goes back to the waiting room and says to the usher:

"I was looking for you. Tell el señor Presidente that I couldn't wait any longer, that if he needs me, he knows where to find me." Cussirat has regained his authoritarian tone.

The usher, admiring someone who treats the marshal with such self-confidence, does not manage a response. He sees how Cussirat puts on his hat, turns half away, and walks off.

"That's how all men ought to be," the Coronel's widow remarks, looking at the olive salesman.

Cussirat steps across the palace threshold and between two Guarupa Indians in shakos, standing guard. Once out on the street, free, he breathes deeply, walks across the Plaza Mayor, looking at the pigeons in the atrium of the cathedral, reaches the Steamboat Café, sits in a wicker chair, and tells the waiter who comes over:

"A café Madrid."

When the waiter walks away, Cussirat lazily puffs on an English Oval, looking at the stone walls of the presidential palace, waiting for the coffee to be brought and for a terrific explosion to crack those walls.


Belaunzarán, bored, unyielding, ill-mannered, awful, says:

"Certainly not."

Doctor Bonilla looks at the other two Moderates in search of some encouraging sign, and does not find it. Disheartened, he then summons his strength and hurls an ultimate, futile charge:

"We Moderates dare to propose that the elections be postponed, thinking that such an arrangement will benefit both parties, and basing ourselves on Article 108 of the Constitution of Arepa."

"Don't go on," declares Belaunzarán. "Article 108 stipulates a joint petition, and the Progressive Party, despite having switched candidates, has not submitted any such petition, which indicates that it does not need extra time to conduct its electoral campaign. I have this information first hand, since I am that candidate and the president of the Party."

"May we submit a petition in writing?" asks Bonilla, to keep up appearances.

"If you wish to waste your time," responds Belaunzarán.

Bonilla stands up, and the others follow suit.

"In that case," Bonilla concludes, "there is nothing more to talk about."

"On that point we are agreed, my good Doctor," responds Belaunzarán, smiling.

With the atmosphere icy, the Moderates bid good-bye, with handshakes and slight bows, to Belaunzarán, who does not get up. Once again they have their little discussion about who goes first and, finally, one behind the other, they leave: Bonilla, Paletón, and the Señor of the Network, who closes the door behind him.

Once alone, Belaunzarán takes a puff and throws his cigar into the spittoon.

At the Steamboat Café, Cussirat, with the café Madrid in front of him, is distressed to see Doctor Malagón, who crosses the street, hailing him:

"Hello there, sportsman!"

And he sits down next to Cussirat.

Belaunzarán pees, paying attention, leaning forward so that his belly does not interfere with his view, with his chin buried in his wattles and his wattles squashed against his chest, his gaze fixed on the tip of his dick. Afterward, he buttons his fly, and then pulls on the chain, with a certain difficulty. He is puzzled upon hearing, instead of water flowing down, a cracking, a breaking of glass, effervescence. He raises his eyes and stares at the water tank. At that moment, like a divine revelation, he sees the explosion. Baam! A flash. The tank breaks in two, the water cascades over Belaunzarán.

With the reactions characteristic of a soldier who has spent part of his life on campaign, Belaunzarán jumps and, prey to panic, flees to his office and dives under the desk. After a while, he realizes that the danger has passed, and, as he recovers, is increasingly enraged.

"Emergency!" he shouts, coming out from under the desk.

Going back to the site of the explosion, he observes the pieces of the water tank, the gush of water hitting the mirror and bouncing off, the flooded floor. He rings the bell next to the toilet.

In the laundry room, the bell rings furiously and on the board the little bulb that says PRESIDENTIAL BATHROOM lights up.

Sebastián, a Negro and an idler, wearing a duck-cloth jacket, wakes up in alarm, gives a jump, grabs a roll of toilet paper, and leaves, running to help the chief.

Belaunzarán returns to his office, calm, in control of himself and the situation. He takes down the mouthpiece of the speaking tube, blows into it, and shouts orders:

"Everyone to combat positions! There's a bomb in the palace! Lock the doors! Seize the three men who are leaving, and if they resist, shoot them!"

He hangs up the speaking tube. Sebastián comes in, agitated, and offers him the roll of toilet paper. Belaunzarán, frantic again, exclaims:

"Treason! A plumber!"

The Guarupas in shakos lock the palace doors. The bugle sounds a call to battle stations. The guards arm themselves. The canvas cover is lifted off the Hotchkiss machine gun, which has never been fired.

The Moderates, grim, not understanding what is going on, ignorant of what awaits them, surprised at the voices giving orders, the soldiers coming and going, and the bugle calls, are crossing the patio toward the vestibule, where a squadron of soldiers stands at attention. The head guard, upon seeing them arrive, orders the sergeant:

"Sergeant, arrest those three!"

The head guard goes to the speaking tube and, while he is communicating with the private office, the sergeant shouts:

"Right flank! Shoulder arms! Arms length to the front! Left face! Squad formation! Halt!"

The Moderates are surrounded in the middle of two rows of soldiers.

"What does this mean?" asks Bonilla.

All the regulars at the Steamboat Café are looking at the closed doors of the palace, and listening to the orders and the call to battle stations.

"What can be going on inside there?" don Gustavo Anzures asks Malagón, who is sitting at the next table.

Malagón dips a lump of sugar in his coffee, takes it out, puts it into his mouth, and, in courtly fashion, answers:

"What must be going on? Larrondo has taken up arms and is going to depose those in power. I'd heard about it already."

Don Gustavo raises his eyebrows and goes from table to table, spreading the word:

"They've seized El Gordo in his den, and they're going to shoot him!"

"The whole thing's a plot hatched in the American Embassy," Malagón explains to Cussirat, who, with great care, is stubbing out a cigarette on a plate.

Duchamps, the reporter for *El Mundo*, abandons his coffee and the companionship of his friends, and goes over to the palace, his notebook ready and his legs trembling.

At the top of the Venetian staircase, surrounded by diligent, terrified henchmen, in control of the situation, Belaunzarán is giving peremptory orders:

"Lock everything up! Every door in the palace with padlocks. You and I have the keys," he says to the superintendent of the palace, who responds with respectful gestures and acts of contrition. He turns to Coronel Larrondo, chief of the presidential guard: "From now on, every person who comes into the palace, straight to the guardroom, and search them head to toe."

"Very well, señor Presidente," responds Larrondo, the presumed ally, standing to attention with a tremendous martial air.

At that moment, the three Moderates are coming up the stairs, disheveled, livid, unkempt, their clothing in disarray, after having been mistreated and stripped of their valuables. A heavy escort accompanies them.

"The guilty parties, sir," announces the official.

As precisely as he has given the previous orders, Belaunzarán gives the following:

"Have Galvazo interrogate them to find out who their accomplices are, and then the firing squad."

"Troops: about face... Right march!" shouts the lieutenant.

Amidst the sweating napes of the escorts, descending the winding stairs like an enormous green worm, appears the disturbed face of Bonilla, who says:

"Mercy! We're innocent!"

At the Steamboat Café a small group has formed around Malagón and Cussirat's table.

"The artillery's in on the plot," says Malagón, in his element, conjecturing, "because this morning I saw the men from the First Company maneuvering a cannon, pulling it into position, with its barrel toward the sappers barracks."

KILL THE LION!

"Martial law will be declared, and we won't be able to go out on the town," says Coco Regalado, who has just arrived.

The idlers of the Steamboat Café, in white suits, striped shirts, celluloid collars, English neckties, imported straw boaters, cufflinks at their wrists, and gold chains across their paunches, force a laugh at Coco Regalado's joke, suck on their cigars, and think, each one of them, about the advantages that will come to them if El Gordo really were captured in his burrow and shot.

At this moment, the death van stops in front of the palace door. Among a crowd of beggars and fried-food vendors, surrounded by the silly escort, the three Moderates are pushed up into the van.

The respectable men in the café do not dare to cross the plaza and so send one of the waiters to investigate.

Duchamps returns with a mouthful of news:

"Somebody placed a bomb in the palace. Nothing happened. El Gordo is running all over. Shouting. They seized the guilty ones and carried them off to the police station to be tortured."

This said, the reporter runs off to *El Mundo*'s editorial office to write up the news for the special edition.

"Damn! Why don't they plot these things better?" says Anzures, in a bad temper.

"And you, Pepe, what do you think of your country?" Coco Regalado asks Cussirat. "Not lacking in excitement, right?"

Cussirat opens his mouth to answer, and stops right there. The cathedral clock strikes two, and only moments after the last peal rings out, like an echo, the little alarm clock inside his briefcase, forgotten on the chair beside Cussirat, starts to ring furiously and muffled.

Confusion, shock, hairs standing on end under the straw hats. Cussirat's hand automatically moves toward the briefcase, halts halfway and pulls back, prudently, coming to rest on its master's trousers.

Don Gustavo Anzures picks up the briefcase and opens it. Malagón, not to be outdone or left behind, puts his hand in and takes out the little clock. He turns to the small group, and in his wisdom explains:

"An alarm clock!"

"Whose briefcase?" Anzures asks.

Coco Regalado, recovered from the shock, is encouraged to say the big joke of the day:

"Sound the alarm! Time to shoot the fools!"

No one laughs.

"Whose briefcase?" Anzures repeats.

No one answers; some of the men go back to their tables, somebody orders a coffee; Cussirat opens his cigarette case and takes out the last English Oval, which he lights with trembling hands, holding it between his tensed lips.

# XIV. Consequences

"Something must be done," says Ángela, with *El Mundo* still in her hands.

Barrientos, Anzures, and Malagón, who have just brought the paper, are standing gloomily in front of her in the music room.

"We came to that conclusion, Ángela," explains Barrientos. "Carlos must intervene. He's Belaunzarán's personal friend."

Ángela stands up.

"It won't do any good," she says. "Carlos thinks he's Belaunzarán's friend, but, actually, he's done nothing more than play dominoes with him on two occasions."

She goes to the telephone in the hall and asks to be put through to Lady Phipps.

"The English Embassy can manage it better, I'm sure," she explains to her friends, before leaving them.

Malagón pulls at his long locks, and dandruff drifts over the shoulders of his checkered suit.

"And there I was, seated at a table in the café, joking! How was I going to imagine that my great friend Paletón was in such a tight fix!"

He walks from one side of the room to the other. Barrientos helps himself to a glass of cognac, which he takes out of a cabinet. Anzures goes over to the window and stands looking out at the peacocks in the light of the setting sun.

"When you get down to it, they deserve it, for handling things so badly. If the bomb had exploded, they'd be holding El Gordo's wake, and we'd be celebrating."

In the hall, Ángela hangs up the minute that Cussirat comes in.

"Pepe," Ángela asks him, "tell me the truth, were you the one?"

Cussirat pretends not to understand.

"Was I the one what?"

"Who placed the bomb in the palace."

With dignified seriousness, Cussirat replies:

"Ángela, if I were to blame, I'd give myself up."

Ángela apologizes:

"Yes, of course. Not for one moment did I think that you'd leave others in a predicament if you were the one who placed the bomb."

"If that were true," Cussirat adds with a touch of irony, "they would shoot the four of us."

They go into the living room together.

"Lord Phipps is at the palace, trying to fix things up," Ángela announces.

Barrientos, limping, seats himself on a settee, from which he reflects out loud, incredulous, while he warms the glass of cognac in his hand.

"What I cannot fathom is how, after fifteen years of talking about good citizenship, such a wild idea could occur to those three."

"So stupid!" concludes Anzures, turning his back to the window.

Ángela reproaches him:

"Gustavo, don't talk like that! Their lives are in danger!"

"What can we do?" asks Cussirat.

"A commission can be formed," says Barrientos unenthusiastically, "signatures collected, clemency begged for . . . but all that takes time. And we don't have it. This has all the earmarks of summary justice. The only thing that can save us is the personal intervention of someone who has influence with that beast."

"Why don't you intervene yourself?" Cussirat asks him.

"I'm just the director of the Bank of Arepa. We're at loggerheads to the bitter end. Why don't you intervene yourself?" Barrientos, in his turn, asks Cussirat.

"Because the day before yesterday he refused to receive me. He stood me up, left me cooling my heels in the antechamber."

"Carlos is the answer," says Barrientos.

"No, why Carlos?" exclaims Malagón, leaving off his pacing. "Another bomb must be hurled!"

"With what object?" asks Anzures.

"So it's seen that we do not agree," Malagón says.

"Who's going to hurl it?" asks Barrientos.

"I would hurl it, with the greatest of pleasure," says Malagón, but giving notice: "if I weren't a political exile."

"One minute," Anzures interrupts. "If someone has the courage to place a bomb, he ought to have the courage to face the consequences. If we intervene, it's for humanity's sake, not out of a sense of obligation."

"Gustavo," Ángela says, "you ought to realize that many of us have thought about doing what these men did, without daring to do it ourselves."

There is a silence. A servant enters.

"Lady Phipps's on the telephone, señora."

Ángela goes out, rapidly, full of hope.

Barrientos laboriously gets up and goes to help himself to another cognac, Malagón following behind him. Anzures returns to looking out the window, Cussirat sits down. Ángela comes back, in despair. They all look at her.

"They've confessed that they're guilty. The English Embassy cannot intervene. They're lost."

All of them grow depressed.

"There's nothing left to do but wait for Carlos," says Barrientos.

They play cards as they wait for don Carlitos. Cussirat wins three games in a row.

When don Carlitos arrives, he comes into the house looking shaken. He stands in the middle of the living room and, tears in his eyes and his arms spread wide, he says:

"They've condemned them to death! They're going to shoot them!"

All the others look at him in consternation.

"You must intercede," Barrientos tells him.

Don Carlitos, from the depths of his unhappiness, answers:

"I already tried to. Useless. They didn't receive me. Ángela, do you realize what this means? With no Moderate deputies in the Chamber, the Law of Expropriation is bearing down upon us, Cumbancha is disappearing right before our eyes ... we're done for."

This said, choking back a sob, walking unsteadily, but raising his head high with dignity, as if he were the man to be shot, don Carlitos leaves the room.

After a moment of silence, Ángela exclaims:

"What a disgrace! Three lives in danger and this man's thinking about his Cumbancha estate!"

She rises and goes after her husband. Cussirat shuffles and deals the cards.

Ángela reaches the second-floor hallway in a flurry of tulle, gasping. She walks toward her husband's bedroom, opens the door and sees him, sitting on the bed, one foot bare, the sock in his hand, and his eyes fixed on the inside of the shoe he just took off.

Ángela calms herself. She enters the room and goes over to the bed. He looks at her and thinks that she is coming to console him. When she comes near, he bursts into tears, leaning his head against his wife's belly. After hesitating, not quite believing it, she lightly strokes his head.

Gaspar, Pereira's cat, sits on the dining room table, posing drowsily for his master, who is sketching his portrait, in pencil, on a drawing pad.

In the living room, Rosita Galvazo, in her underskirt, looks at herself in the mirror. Esperanza takes a final stitch in the flowery percale she is trying to make fit over fleshy curves of her friend and client. Doña Soledad, sitting in a rocking chair, feeds the recently born canary perched on her fist, which is resting in her lap, by sticking a tooth pick moistened with foul glop into the bird's open beak: she utters a celebrated phrase:

"In my day, things were different," and then, addressing the canary, she tells it: "Eat, stupid, your mother's not here. Who could ever have imagined, at six in the afternoon, a grown man, sitting in the dining room, drawing a portrait of his cat? In the old days, men got drunk, but they brought home the money."

Rosita, contemplating her plumpness, remarks:

"I'm getting fatter by the day! Good thing Galvazo likes it that way."

Esperanza, her mouth full of pins, stands up, spreads out the dress, which is vast, and says between her teeth:

"It's only basted."

"How charming! How elegant! How distinguished!" doña Soledad comments, distractedly picking at the canary's eye.

Rosita puts on the dress, which Esperanza tries to pull down over her buttocks.

Galvazo, satisfied, with packages of food in his arms, brimming over with good humor, enters the house and rushes into the living room without saying a word to anyone. The women, between coquettish giggles, shout:

"Oh God! the enemy!"

"Shut your eyes, you demon!"

"Out, you snoop!"

Galvazo, the Terror of Police Headquarters, shuts his eyes, affecting modesty, as though he had never seen his wife in her underwear, and allows Esperanza and Rosita, between the two of them, to turn him around and push him to the door, saying:

"Into the dining room, big guy, you've got no business in here!"

Doña Soledad, tilting back her head and the rocking chair, the canary still perched on her fist, lets out a belly laugh, enjoying the questionable, puritanical moment.

Pedro Galvazo bursts into the dining room, waking up Gaspar and drying up his master's creative juices. As Gaspar jumps down from the table and escapes into the kitchen and Pereira covers his drawing with a blank sheet, Galvazo puts the packages on the table and says:

"A real rough day, but productive."

"What did you do?"

"Nothing less than finish off the opposition!"

"Which opposition?"

"Your boss, don Casimiro."

Pereira grows alarmed.

"Don Casimiro? What happened?"

"He tried to assassinate the president. Him, and two others. Luckily, they failed. They were nabbed and brought to me.

They didn't want to confess, the cowards. I grabbed don Casimiro, 'Kneel down for me,' I said to him. I gave him a shove in the you-know-where. Good God! All three confessed. They'll be shot tomorrow."

Pereira changes color.

"Going to shoot don Casimiro? Going to close the Institute? How am I going to earn my living?"

"With that little guitar you play."

"But that doesn't bring in enough."

"Look, don't be so egotistical. Think what this means for the country: with the Moderate opposition done for, the political atmosphere is going to stay cleaner than a freshly laundered shirt. Now, we're really going to live in peace."

Pereira, unable to concentrate on the advantages brought about by the Moderates' disappearance, plunged into grief, rakes his hand through his hair. Galvazo tries to console him:

"Don't worry, you have well-to-do friends who'll help you."

He wraps his arm around the other man's shoulders. Pereira looks up at him, worried, but pleased by the display of friendship. Galvazo, seeing that his friend's concern is lessening, withdraws his arm, opens the packages on the table and says:

"Now we're going to think about eating."

He sets a can to one side and shows it to Pereira, who watches him sadly, and says:

"Know what this is? *Pâtè de foie gras.* The most delicious thing you'll ever eat. We snatched it as contraband. Got some bread?"

The following day, Bonilla, Paletón, and the Señor of the Network got up early, performed their necessities in front of the guard on duty, shaved with a borrowed blade, made their confession to Padre Inastrillas, walked down the halls of the police headquarters between a squad of mounted police officers, and stood in the service patio, with their backs to the target-practice wall, watching how the mounted police knelt, cut the cartridges' wrappers, aimed, and fired. They died at daybreak.

Attending the execution were Jiménez, wrapped in a Prussian cape that made him sweat buckets; Galvazo, wide awake after a sleepless night; a minister of the Supreme Court, who was the official witness; Cardona, representing the office of the president and with orders to make sure the guilty ones were really dead; Padre Inastrillas, who gave the benediction; and several reporters and photographers.

The *coup de grâce* was left to Lieutenant Ibarra, a shady character, who will never again appear in this story, or in any other, because he died that same night from alcoholic congestion.

# xv. New Directions

The burial was simple but moving. Everyone who attended agreed that Bonilla, Paletón, and the Señor of the Network had died for a just cause —"to liberate Arepa from the tyrant" — and afterward they went home, to grumble privately against the new martyrs, who, by their clumsiness, had succeeded only in terminating opposition in the Chamber, provoking Belaunzarán's wrath, and putting their supporters in a tight spot.

For fifteen days no one stopped in at the casino for fear of being accused of complicity in the attempted assassination. Some, like don Carlitos, were sick in bed, reading, shaking in his boots, *El Mundo*, expecting news of the Law of Expropriation's being unanimously approved in the Chamber and put into effect. Others, like Barrientos, locked themselves in their offices to examine ways of investing abroad. Pepe Cussirat went to the country, shotgun in hand, to hunt rabbits, which turned out to be easier to kill than the marshal, but less so than the Moderates. Ángela spent the fifteen days grieving deeply for the deceased, disillusioned with the living, and dedicating her energies to organizing an evening of poetry to commemorate Paletón as well as raise an endowment for the Krauss Institute, and to ordering the servants to prepare her husband's broth and serve it promptly. Pepita Jiménez went on waiting in vain for Cussirat to speak of marriage. Pereira, thanks to the endowment, did not lose his job.

KILL THE LION!

At the end of the fifteen days, the truce is over and things are taking unexpected directions. Belaunzarán, with the enemy in his fist, has new plans.

By means of a messenger and a message in his own hand, he invites don Carlitos, Barrientos, and Bartolomé González to dine at his La Chacota estate.

Don Carlitos gets up out of bed and takes a bath, Barrientos comes out of his office, and don Bartolomé calls for a meeting of the invited in order to decide whether the invitation should be accepted or not. They meet at Barrientos's office.

"Will he want to shoot us too?" don Carlitos asks.

The other two calm him down. For that, Belaunzarán does not need to invite them to dinner, it is enough to call in the troops.

"I think we ought to go," ventures don Bartolomé González. "I'm prepared to sell him my soul, just so he doesn't take away my money."

"What's more," says Barrientos, "we have no other alternative. I don't dare to refuse an invitation from El Gordo."

In point of fact, the conclave is good only for agreeing on what they should wear.

"I'm going dressed in white, with a Panama hat," don Carlitos wants them to know.

When they arrive at La Chacota, all three together in the González Rolls, the marshal, in boots and country clothes, is waiting for them on the porch of the Moorish house, greets them cordially, shows them the cockpit, and, once back in the house, introduces them to his wife, Gregorita, who has a moustache, one glass eye, and never appears in public, as well as to his daughters, Rufina and Tadifa, who are famous for never having opened their mouths except to laugh at some bit of nonsense.

After introductions, the women withdraw, the men sip an aperitif on the porch overlooking the park (protected from strangers by a battalion of presidential guards), loosen up, let down their guard, eat, the four of them alone, roast suckling pig in a summer house, and now, with the after-dinner talk, Belaunzarán opens fire, or better said, puts his cards on the table.

"I want to assure you, I am the first in lamenting the deaths of the Moderates," Belaunzarán says.

"And we're second," says Barrientos, in order to agree with the marshal and also to defend his territory.

They all agree: Bonilla, Paletón, and the Señor of the Network forced the marshal to execute them, and in doing that he was only doing his duty, preserving the country's peace and saving the institutions.

"Aside from the significant loss we have suffered with the death of these people," Belaunzarán says, "there remains the void they leave in the Chamber. The Moderate Party goes unrepresented."

The others agree: that is one of their main concerns, they grant.

"The Chamber has been left unbalanced," Belaunzarán says. "A heated debate could lead to the approval of laws that are prejudicial for some group or social class."

They all agree with him, without knowing very well what ground they are treading.

"In order to resolve this situation," proceeds the marshal (the others holding their breath), "it has occurred to me that, perhaps, the most expeditious solution would be for me, personally, to appoint three substitutes . . . "

Silence. Belaunzarán goes on:

"They could, of course, count on the support and confidence of the Moderate Party."

Approval.

"Have you thought of any names, señor Presidente?" Barrientos asks very cautiously.

"Yes, señor Barrientos," Belaunzarán replies, "I've thought of names. Your three names."

The three chosen men heave a sigh of relief, look at each other, smile, agree.

"I believe selecting you has been the right choice," Belaunzarán concludes.

Everyone agrees. Belaunzarán proceeds, outlining his plan:

"Once you are in the Chamber and balance is restored, you three will have the opportunity to do many things, among them the following: to draft a law that ratifies the property rights of every Arepan citizen, regardless of his origin or descent."

Jaws drop. The idea is too good to be accepted without discussion. Don Bartolomé sees the flaw:

"But we are only three. The proposal will have seven votes against."

Amused, Belaunzarán speaks frankly:

"If I propose an idea to you, señor González, it's because I believe it's viable. I'll see to it that the Progressive deputies vote for the Law of Ratification of Patrimony, as the one I'm outlining might be called."

Contained joy. His interlocutors look at each other, speechless with delight at the imminent death of the Law of Expropriation.

"Do you think we can work together?" Belaunzarán asks them.

"Yes, sir!" rings out in three voices. Belaunzarán continues:

"Perfect. Once the Law of Ratification of Patrimony is approved, you'll have to do me a favor. Are you prepared to do me a favor?"

"Whatever you ask of us," says don Carlitos.

"Always and if it is within our scope," Barrientos warns.

"And is not prejudicial to anyone," González adds, thinking about his pesos.

Belaunzarán reassures them:

"It's within your possibilities, and is not prejudicial to anyone."

He shoots to kill:

"It's very simple. It consists of proposing the creation of the Presidency for Life."

Silence. Dejection. Distrust. Stammering. Belaunzarán sets forth his reasons:

"Progress is essential for the nation. For progress, stability is essential. We will achieve stability, with you holding on to your properties and me to the presidency. All together, all content, and forward."

"I'm in complete agreement with you, señor Presidente," says don Carlitos.

"I'm glad, señor Berriozábal," says Belaunzarán and he warns the other two:

"Without the Presidency for Life, things will be more difficult. The Law of Ratification of Patrimony, for instance, won't have the best chance for passage in the Chamber."

Barrientos and don Bartolomé González fold their hands, accept Belaunzarán's proposition, and toast the new alliance with him.

"Something else that would be advisable," says Belaunzarán, wiping cognac from his lips after the toast, "is for the Moderate Party, which has no candidate for president, to nominate me."

Silence again. Belaunzarán continues his explanation:

"That way, we kill two birds with one stone. The Moderate Party will be able to share in my victory, and we avoid the danger, very remote, of the lifetime presidency falling into the hands of some unknown."

"I am in complete agreement with you, señor Presidente," don Carlitos says again.

"I'm glad, señor Berriozábal," Belaunzarán says again. "And what about you?" he asks, turning to the other two.

"We are Moderates, señor Mariscal," Barrientos explains, "but we are not the Party."

"You are distinguished members," Belaunzarán says. "I'm convinced that you can present me to the others, proposing me as the candidate, and explaining to your colleagues the advantages that can derive from this arrangement. On the other hand, since I believe that this is fundamental, if there's no candidacy, there's no deal."

Don Carlitos stands up and says:

"Señor Presidente, you can count on me. I will give a party for you in my house, present you to all the members of the casino, and that way you'll have the opportunity to speak with them, to see what their expectations are, and to study their problems. I'm certain my colleagues, here present, will help us, you and me, in this task of convincing the others."

They all agree, another toast, end of the meeting.

On their way back, Barrientos asks don Carlitos:

"And your wife, who doesn't back away from calling El Gordo an assassin, she's going to receive him in her home?"

Don Carlitos, who has been thinking about the same thing, does not respond. He mops his brow with a handkerchief.

# xvi. Convincing Ángela

"First, Padre Inastrillas will introduce," Ángela, in her *boudoir*, instructs Pepita Jiménez, "then, you read the fragments; then, comes Malagón's speech, which he's already written and is very interesting; when the speech is over, intermission, and in the second half of the program, the 'Ode to Democracy,' which you must rehearse carefully, because it's one of Casimiro's most moving works and the last he wrote. To end, the tableau Conchita's putting on with a corps of schoolgirls, and which I hope turns out well. We can't count on Gustavo. He flatly refuses to take part in the evening. He's afraid. It's a pity, because he has such a beautiful voice ... What's the matter?"

Pepita, listless and emaciated, has not paid attention. She is crying. Ángela, understanding, takes Pepita's hand.

"It's Pepe you're crying about?" she asks.

Pepita cries more. When the tears stop, the hiccups begin. Ángela waits patiently for her answer.

"Ángela, such heartache. He's polite, but not affectionate. He hasn't said a word to me about what I want to hear. He almost doesn't look at me, and when he does, it's as if he no longer remembers ... about ... all that."

Ángela gets up from the Louis XVI chair, goes to her dressing table, selects a chocolate, eats it, and offers the box to Pepita, while she expresses this thought:

"Unfortunately, Pepita, we have no command over other people's minds. These things, when they happen, and, sadly, they do happen, we have to accept them and move ahead."

"But I'm thirty-five, Ángela. I gave my youth to this man."

"Because you wanted to. Don't reproach him."

"His letters were so affectionate!"

"But how long has it been since he left off writing to you?"

Pepita lowers her eyes and swallows the chocolate before answering:

"Twelve years."

"You see? You didn't forget him, but you can't ask the same of a man. You're being unfair to him."

Pepita raises her eyes and fixes them on Ángela's face.

"You think there's no hope?"

Ángela, ill at ease, decides to be frank:

"Apparently none at all."

Pepita, facing the confirmation of her suspicions, thinks it over:

"I was resigned. I was happy. But now, his being here ... has hurt me a lot."

Pepita starts crying again, and Ángela takes her hand. Then, seeing that the tears do not stop, she gets up, slightly impatient, and says:

"All right. It's time for us to go to the committee meeting."

Ángela, Pepita, Conchita Parmesano, Malagón, and Padre Inastrillas have an appointment with Bertoletti, director of the Puerto Alegre Opera, to see about décor. Pepita stops crying.

"Dry that face," Ángela commands.

Pepita Jiménez goes into the bathroom. Ángela, alone, looks at herself in the mirror and pats the skin of her cheek.

Don Carlitos, gotten up to the nines, like a spiffy little tick, climbs the stairs in short leaps, full of decisiveness, of hopes, of ideas that he thinks brilliant, that have just occurred to him in the casino bar with the aid of Barrientos and don Bartolomé González, and also knowing the risk he is running, the danger that Ángela will send him packing when he asks her to give a party for Belaunzarán—and prepared to lie.

In this animated state, he reaches the hallway on the second floor. He goes to the door of his wife's *boudoir*, pauses for a moment, preparing the words he will use to open his plea, and signals with a knock, coquettishly.

"Come in!"

Don Carlitos goes in. Seeing Ángela and Pepita ready to go out on the street, wearing hats and necklaces, he is disconcerted.

"You're drunk," says Ángela.

"Not true. I had one drink, no more."

"We're going to a committee meeting at the theater," Ángela says, pulling on a glove, putting an end to the conversation.

Don Carlitos could not care less where his wife is going. Seeing his plan in danger, he decides to go on the offensive:

"Angelita, I've come to ask you a favor."

"I don't have time to do any favors," Ángela says, "I'm going out."

"And I don't have time to wait for your return," answers don Carlitos, and adds, addressing Pepita: "Dear, cover your ears, she and I have to talk privately for a moment."

Ángela, facing the inevitable, tells Pepita:

"Wait for me downstairs."

When Pepita has left, don Carlitos draws close to his wife and tells her, as if in secret:

"There's still hope!"

"Of what?" she asks.

"Of saving Cumbancha. But I need your help. To be frank, I need you to save me."

Ángela, severe, asks her husband:

"What are you plotting?"

Don Carlitos, pretending to be delighted, like someone announcing the best news of the century, says:

"Belaunzarán wants to become a member of the casino!"

He takes a step back to see what effect these words have on his wife. She is not moved.

"And what's that to me?"

Don Carlitos does not lose heart. He again takes up the charge, with the second part of his lie:

"I hope you're listening to this: the board of directors has convened to discuss his application, and they have rejected it."

"Well done!" says Ángela.

Don Carlitos puts up a hand to halt his wife's righteous approval and continues:

"Don't proclaim victory, until you've heard the end. Belaunzarán has been rejected, not as an assassin, as you call him, not as a mulatto, as others call him," and he again steps back as though aiming to give the *coup de grâce*. "His application was rejected because he didn't meet an indispensable formality: it didn't come accompanied by a sponsoring letter from a founding member. Belaunzarán has done me the honor, think of it! of requesting that I be the one who recommends him, do you understand?"

Ángela looks at him as at a nonentity, and tells him, disheartened:

"Yes, I understand. You're going to recommend him."

Don Carlitos draws near to his wife.

"Of course! Not only am I going to recommend him, I'm going to present him in society!" He takes his wife's gloved hand between his own, and adds: "If you agree."

Ángela looks at him with astonished distrust.

"What are you saying?"

"The 13th of July is the anniversary of the Battle of Rebenco. We'll hold a dance here in the house, invite the *crème de la crème* of Arepa, and then God himself cannot take Cumbancha away from us."

Ángela is aghast.

"Here, in this house? Belaunzarán in this house?"

Don Carlitos grows anxious.

"Say yes, Angelita! Make a sacrifice! In the end, when all's said and done, it's only for one night! Say yes!"

He tries to kiss Ángela's glove, but she pulls back her hand violently.

"You're crazy!"

She goes to the door. Don Carlitos, desperate, goes down on his knees.

"Ángela, I beg you, on my knees!"

Ángela leaves the room, not even turning to look back at him and see him kneeling, with his arms outspread, almost drooling. When he sees that all is lost, don Carlitos rises to his feet, with much greater effort than what kneeling cost him. Then, he goes to his room and sits, for hours, in an armchair, staring into space.

Between her house and the theater, Ángela keeps her mouth shut, furious, looking down at the road. At the theater, while Conchita and Bertoletti discuss the décor, she gets an idea. She returns to her house in a good mood, goes up to her husband's room, enters without knocking, finds him still sitting in the armchair, dejected, and gives him a surprise:

"I've changed my mind. Yes, we're going to give a party for Belaunzarán."

Don Carlitos almost dies from joy.

KILL THE LION!

"Thank you, Ángela, thank you," he says to her, kissing his wife's hands.

She looks at him in silence, as though amused by his happiness. He, thankful and innocent, goes on kissing his wife's hands, without even suspecting the dark ideas floating in her brain.

# xvii. Other Plans

At ten in the morning, Cussirat, in pajamas and silk robe, with a hairnet over his head, flattening his hair, is eating his breakfast on the terrace, looking at the wooded patio. Garatuza, after taking away the plate with vague traces of fillet and potatoes, serves him coffee and hands him the newspaper.

On the front page of *El Mundo* appears the photograph of Belaunzarán, hurtling a shuttle, very clumsily, on its first travels across a loom, thus inaugurating Arepa's first spinning and textile factory, founded with French capital. The inauguration took place the previous day, before—and the paper does not state this—the fat cats' dinner.

After assuring himself that nothing more is to be served and leaving his boss absorbed in reading the daily foolishnesses out in the cool of the patio, Garatuza retires to the kitchen and prepares to eat breakfast.

The Berriozábal's Dion-Button stops on calle de Cordobanes, in front of the Cussirats' house. The chauffeur, sweating inside his livery, gets out of the car, goes up to the front door, and pounds twice with the knocker, which reverberates in the vestibule and causes Garatuza, who is in the kitchen eating tripe, to jump up, wipe his lips with a piece of bread, and run down the stairs while simultaneously rolling down his sleeves.

"Señora Berriozábal wishes to see señor Cussirat," the chauffeur announces, bowing slightly at each of the names.

Garatuza is speechless, stiffens, looks into the car, sees that his leg is not being pulled, since Ángela, reserved, wearing a hat and dangling earrings, is in the back seat, looking at him. He suppresses his sense of scandal and says to the chauffeur:

"I'll go announce her."

Ángela, dressed as for a visit to the nuns, sits beside Cussirat on the terrace, takes a sip from the *demi tasse* in front of her, puts the napkin to her lips for an instant, and says:

"Malagón proposes throwing a bomb to demonstrate solidarity with the martyrs. I don't believe that's the way. I believe that the best homage we can pay to our dead friends is to carry out the enterprise for which they sacrificed their lives."

Cussirat sits up straight in his chair, ill at ease, looking at his visitor, as at an intruder, and tells her:

"Ángela, this is my mission. I promise you, I'll know how to carry it out."

"I'm sure of that. I haven't come to reproach you but, on the contrary: I come to ask you to lead us."

Cussirat looks at her without understanding.

"What do you mean, lead *us*? Lead who?"

Ángela leans her arms on the table and speaks with precise vehemence:

"I was awake all night, thinking about what's taken place in Arepa lately. It's evident that you're not the only one who thinks the moment has come for finishing off Belaunzarán."

Cussirat beats a retreat and takes refuge in a feigned meditation. Ángela goes on:

"You already made one attempt, our friends made another.

Don't you think that if they'd been in cahoots with you they'd have achieved better results?"

"If they had been in cahoots, your friends wouldn't have gone to the palace."

Ángela mistakes the intention of his words:

"Exactly. You're the only man on this island who has sufficient intelligence, courage, and decisiveness to carry out this undertaking."

Cussirat lowers his eyes, ashamed.

"Up until this moment, I've failed," he says.

Ángela hurls herself into the attack:

"Because what you did was rash: you might not have gotten out of the palace alive, since you were alone. But what happened holds a great lesson: God didn't want your attempt to be successful, but Divine Providence is on our side, because you're alive. The moment has come to call together all the people who are ready to sacrifice themselves for their country, to form a group with them, train them, organize them, and carry out the undertaking. You're the right person to head such a group."

"Don't count me in," Cussirat says.

"Why not?"

Cussirat, uncomfortable, shies away from his visitor's gaze and waits a minute before answering:

"Because it's dangerous to work in a group. It can be infiltrated, there can be gaffes, blunders . . . "

"Don't be arrogant! Don't be an egotist! What's going to happen if you fail? Who's going to pick up your work? Let us collaborate with you. Allow us to help you and protect you! Don't deny us a little of your glory!"

Cussirat, embarrassed and annoyed, stops her short:

"Ángela, please!"

Frustrated, she falls silent. Her eyes brim over with tears, her lips tremble, and her breathing grows agitated. Her passion is ridiculous but impressive. Cussirat is intimidated, she sees that, and, swiping with a paw, seizes the man's hand, defenseless and cornered as he is in his seat, and says to him:

"Please, you! You, please!"

She presses his hand between hers. Cussirat, perplexed, feeling ridiculous in his hairnet, trying to rescue his hand and put an end to the scene, says:

"What are you proposing?"

In tears, she smiles at him, triumphant and grateful. He makes an effort, timid and unsuccessful, to withdraw his hand.

"Luck's on our side," Ángela says, smiling, triumphant. "Belaunzarán will be coming to my home within the month."

Cussirat looks at her, interested, forgetting, for the moment, about his hand.

Pepita Jiménez, dark circles under her eyes, hair done primly, downcast and pale; but her lips painted cherry red, and dressed in see-through black, while standing center stage and wearing shoes too big for her, gestures with her bare arms and, tinkling her bracelets, recites, in a plaintive voice, the last lines of Paletón's poem:

> Embittered heart,
> Abandoned heart,
> Where are you going?

"Oh, it's a work of art!" comments Conchita Parmesano, from the third row, and claps her hands.

The other people attending the rehearsal also applaud.

Cussirat, at Ángela's side, in the middle of the orchestra, gestures impatiently and says:

"That woman will never do."

Ángela looks at him reproachfully.

"She's very brave, and she loves you a lot," she tells him.

"Which are two virtues that have nothing to do with the ability to assassinate presidents. Absolutely, that woman, *out!*"

"Pepe!" Ángela says, as though wanting to put an end to the insults. Deep in her heart, Cussirat's bad opinion of Pepita flatters her, because she knows that it does not apply to her.

Cussirat, scowling, looks around the theater.

"Which one's Pereira?"

Pepita has gone to sit next to the Regalados. The girls from the academy go up onto the back of the stage, and, obeying contradictory commands from Bertoletti and Conchita Parmesano, fall into formation after several false starts. Padre Inastrillas, extending his arms, pays an edifying compliment to the poetess; don Carlitos, slumped down in his seat, waits, patiently, for the rehearsal to end; Malagón, near the proscenium, takes advantage of the footlights' brightness to read his speech and scratch his crotch; Lady Phipps comes in just at that moment from the bathroom, pulling down her slip; Pereira stands in the aisle at the back of the theater with his arms crossed, watching, respectfully, the confusion up on the stage.

Ángela signals to him with a movement of her head. Cussirat stands up, excuses himself to don Carlitos, and, smiling, steps past Pepita, stumbles past Padre Inastrillas, walks up the aisle, and approaches Pereira, who, seeing him come near, has turned pale.

"Where did you learn to play the violin?" Cussirat asks.

Pereira is startled.

"Me?"

Cussirat understands that he has been too brusque and decides to tell him a lie in order to boost his confidence:

"I ask, because you do it so well."

Pereira smiles, flattered.

"Here, in Puerto Alegre. Señor Quiroz, who directs the orchestra where I work, taught me."

Cussirat, to whom the answer is of no interest, only the reaction of the man he has questioned, feigns surprise.

"You don't say! That's impressive! I'd have thought that you studied abroad."

"No, señor, I have never been off Arepa."

Seeing his subject at ease, Cussirat puts a hand on his shoulder and says to him:

"Come, we have to talk."

They walk down the aisle, Pereira yet more flattered, Cussirat looking down at the floor, as though carefully thinking over what he is going to say.

"What do you think of the political situation?"

Pereira looks at him in surprise.

"Nothing at all, Engineer."

Cussirat stops and rivets his eyes on him. Pereira grows uneasy.

"What do you mean?" he asks.

"I mean, what do you think of the executions?"

Pereira takes a moment to answer.

"Well, someone who knows told me the shootings were a good thing. That the political atmosphere is going to be a lot clearer. So they say, because I, personally, had nothing against don Casimiro Paletón, since he'd always been very good to me. Well, not very good, but not bad either."

Cussirat continues looking at him for a moment, then smiles and says:

"That's an interesting opinion, good-bye."

Leaving Pereira perplexed, he moves away from him, in the

direction of where he was sitting before. Seating himself next to Ángela, Cussirat tells her:

"That man is an idiot."

"That's what my son says," Ángela answers indifferently.

# XVIII. The Assassins' Dinner

At night, in the living room of the Cussirats' old house, among sofas in dust covers and alabasters in storage, the chosen ones gather. Malagón, scratching his thick mane of hair; Paco Ridruejo, in dandified attire, moving freely through his friend's house; Anzures, sitting rigid on the edge of a chair upholstered in brushed brocade; and Barrientos, sipping an aperitif. Cussirat, well dressed in the middle of the room, with his hand resting on the tortoise-shell tabletop, is warning them:

"This will not be a social gathering. We're going to discuss very serious matters. Then dinner will be brought in from the English Hotel."

The guests look at him, more intrigued than at the start.

The pounding doorknocker resounds.

"It's Ángela," says Cussirat, leaving the room.

He is trotting nimbly down the stairs when he stops, astonished, upon seeing Ángela and Pepita Jiménez in the vestibule.

The women start coming up, and they meet their host at the midpoint of the stairs.

"Pepe," says Pepita on coming up next to him, "thank you for inviting me to your dinner."

Tense, Cussirat shakes her hand, feigning friendliness and a smile, and when she continues on her way up to the top of the stairs, he says to Ángela, severe, in lowered tones:

"Why did you bring her?"

"Because there was no way around it," Ángela answers, also in a lowered voice. "She met Malagón in the street, and he told her you were giving a dinner. She came to my house awash in tears."

"I told you there would always be gaffes!" Cussirat says.

After this exchange, the two of them, their smiles frozen, continue on their way up to the top, where Pepita Jiménez is waiting for them, looking around sadly, deeply breathing in the house's stale air.

"All this brings back such memories to me!" she says.

Cussirat leads her into the living room. On the threshold, just before going in, Pepita takes a bundle of papers out of her handbag and gives it to Cussirat.

"Here, take this. It's a poem I wrote while thinking about you."

Feigning, not only his smile but also his pleasure, Cussirat stuffs the bundle into his pocket and lets Pepita precede him into the room, where the others, standing up, have greeted Ángela.

"Hello there, beautiful," Malagón says, opening his arms wide on seeing Pepita come in.

The beginning of the dinner was a disaster. Cussirat had to pretend that he was reading the 123 passionate lines written by Pepita, while he deliberated, deep down, if he would go ahead with the plan as devised. Ángela removed his indecision when she said:

"Say what you have to say to us."

Then, Cussirat, like someone diving head first into a well, explained the purpose of the gathering.

After the dinner, solemn, as though they had just heard the Sermon on the Mount, the new conspirators listened to Cussirat's last warning:

"Anyone who's not in agreement with these basics, should leave now."

Barrientos, on whom the plan and the dinner have weighed like a stone, is on the point of leaving, but is held back by the thought that if the conspiracy succeeds and they kill the marshal, his getting up from the table at this juncture is going to constitute an unpardonable offense. For a moment he thinks about the possibility of explaining to everyone present the new agreement he has reached with Belaunzarán, but as he knows he cannot be reasoning with the idealists (and that is what Ángela and Cussirat, at least, really are), he decides to keep his mouth shut.

Anzures, cursing the moment when he accepted the invitation to dine, says that he agrees. Paco Ridruejo and Pepita Jiménez, truly moved by the prospects, also agree.

Malagón takes the floor:

"My dear sportsman, remember that I am a man without a country. This land has given me asylum, and I don't want to violate its laws."

"Your advice, Doctor," Cussirat says, "can be of inestimable value."

"If we're talking about advice," Malagón says, "then I'm staying."

The tension lessens. Everybody laughs, good-naturedly. Paco Ridruejo asks:

"All right, we all agree, but what's to be done?"

"Ángela has a plan," Cussirat says.

Ángela explains: the 13th of July, at her house, a party for Belaunzarán—and his death. Everyone is invited.

"July 13th?" asks Anzures. "That leaves very little time."

"Rubbish!" says Malagón. "If there's enough time to make arrangements for a dance, there's enough to make arrangements for an assassination."

"Don't speak that word, Doctor," Ángela says, "this will be tyrannicide."

Ángela looks at Cussirat and he at her, approvingly. Barrientos, for his part, thinks: "Damn! What was going to be our triumph is going to be our downfall!"

Ángela, sticking to her role, continues authoritatively:

"I have to warn you about one thing: I want no bloodshed."

"Agreed," Malagón says, "I'll administer belladonna."

"What will we give it to him in?" asks Paco Ridruejo.

"Cognac," says Barrientos, "he's a heavy drinker."

"Unfortunately," says Cussirat, "he's not the only one. The smallest slip could produce a massacre."

"Never that, ever! Not for one moment should the lives of my guests be in danger," Ángela begs.

"All right," Malagón says, "let's think of something else."

"I have an idea," says Pepita Jiménez, blushing.

Everyone looks at her with interest, except for Cussirat, who is made uneasy.

"It comes from a novel by Mauricio Balzán," Pepita says, somewhat pedantically, citing Mauricio Balzán as an authority. "The heroine's armed with a syringe filled with a terribly lethal substance, and the villain is injected with it."

"Of course!" says Malagón. "That's the solution!"

"Do you know of a substance with these properties, doctor?" asks Barrientos, interested.

"A substance! There are dozens!" exclaims the doctor referred to, explaining: "Extract of *apraxia algida*, sublimate of *acido thymonucleincia*, a 10% solution of *cramberia vertiginosa*, and, the easiest to procure, curare. The Guarupas still use it to hunt boars."

"Wait a minute," says Cussirat. "The substances exist, I agree, but they're hard to administer. We're not going to ask Belaunzarán to give himself an injection."

"But it's a dance, Cussirat, my friend," Anzures reminds him, in his haste to put the death onto the ladies. "Belaunzarán has to dance, and one good pin prick . . ."

"Anybody might excuse that," concludes Malagón.

"But it takes courage and nerves of steel to dance with someone and, smiling, give him a shot of something you know is fatal," says Cussirat.

"I'm in agreement there," Barrientos, says, "it's difficult."

For a moment the gathering waivers. Pepita Jiménez speaks up: "I'm ready to do it."

Anzures heaves a sigh of relief; Cussirat, exasperated, falls silent; Paco Ridruejo looks at Pepita with curiosity for the first time in his life. Malagón exclaims:

"Blessed be the mother who gave birth to you, Pepita! You're one of my kind."

Ángela says to Cussirat:

"See? It wasn't such a bad idea for her to come."

Cussirat does not back down:

"And what happens if Belaunzarán doesn't feel like dancing with Pepita? We'll miss our chance."

Malagón comes to the poetess's defense:

"Come on, man, the woman's pretty. What are you thinking about? What she did to you, she can do to anyone! At the blink of an eye, this girl can hook not only a marshal but a whole army!"

Pepita looks at Cussirat, her eyes fluttering spectacularly. He gives in. He asks Malagón:

"And this substance you're talking about, it can be gotten hold of?"

"I'll see to that myself," Malagón says.

Cussirat looks around the room.

"Everybody agrees?"

KILL THE LION!

No one says no. Cussirat, looking down at the tablecloth and fidgeting uncomfortably, says:

"All right then. We'll do as we've said, we'll arrange the details later."

Ángela extends her arm toward Pepita, who is sitting across from her, and touches her hand, in a gesture of congratulation.

"I think we require a toast," says Barrientos.

At that, the gathering grows lively, everyone speaks at once, except for Pepita, who is looking at Cussirat, who avoids her eyes.

## xix. Face to Face with Death?

Flying at high altitude, in the clean morning air, Cussirat's plane drones and seems to hang suspended above the Bay of Alcanfores. From the front cabin and into the strong wind, Tintín Berriozábal pokes out his head to take a look at the blue sea, the crystalline shoals, the breaking surf, the golden sands of the beach, and the blackish coconut groves. Unhurried, the plane leaves the sea behind and, approaching the first spurs of the mountain, flies over some tobacco growers, who gape at it; crossing the other slope, the plane drops down and heads toward Ventosa, circling over the plain, steadily descending and, roaring, passes a few meters above Ángela's and Pepita Jiménez's parasols, finally landing, with a bounce, before the startled eyes of the two women.

Tintín gets out trembling and vomits on the ground, helped by his mother, who supports his forehead with her hand, her arm stretched out in order not to stain herself.

Cussirat, taking off his goggles, joins Pepita.

"You had bad weather?" asks the poetess.

"How could we have had bad weather? Aren't you looking at the calmest day ever?"

The poetess shrinks back and makes an excuse:

"I thought it was different up there. That there were storms a person wasn't aware of on the ground."

"You thought wrong. It's exactly the same."

She searches his eyes.

"Pepe, what do you have against me?"

Cussirat, who has been looking at the Blériot, realizes that his brusqueness has gone too far, and tones himself down.

"Against you? Nothing at all. Why would I have anything against you? On the contrary," he kisses her on the cheek.

But she does not let herself be convinced.

"Then why haven't you spoken to me about marriage? If you want to go back on your promises, I'll leave you free to do that."

The barrier separating Cussirat from exasperation breaks down and he says:

"How can I go talking to you about marriage, when tomorrow you're going to try to kill a man? It's not the time to talk about the future. We are face to face with death."

She looks at him, her eyes round, understanding that this is the end of the engagement. He, full of dissatisfaction, repenting of what he has just said, and not daring to admit it, draws away from her, walks over to Garatuza, who stands alongside the plane, and gives him instructions.

Ángela, after wiping her son's mouth with her handkerchief, puts her arm around his shoulders and leads him to the Dussemberg. On the way she stops in surprise upon seeing the poetess's tragic face.

"What's the matter?" she asks.

Pepita Jiménez shakes her head, without answering.

Ángela looks at her, full of apprehension.

The syringe looks like a tiepin: a slender hypodermic, mounted on a pear-shaped pearl, pinkish, huge, and fake, containing the ampoule of poison.

"You stick it in, and then squeeze," Malagón explains to Pepita, exhibiting the tiepin with a craftsman's pride. "A second is long enough. The poison acts quickly. Before he realizes that you've pricked him, he'll be on the floor. I'll state that he had an attack. The investigations will come later."

He hands the ampoule to her ceremoniously. They are in Ángela's *boudoir*, dressed to kill: Ángela in floor-length black with *aigrettes* on her head, Pepita in a borrowed gown, Cussirat in a trim-cut tuxedo, and Malagón bursting at the seams and smelling of mothballs.

"Good luck," says Malagón.

Ángela takes the tiepin from Pepita and, with nervous fingers, pins it on the poetess's low-necked gown.

"You'll have it right at hand here," she tells her.

"Will you have the courage to stick it in?" Cussirat asks, worried.

Ángela comes to Pepita's defense.

"What questions you ask, Pepe! Of course she'll have the courage!"

Pepita is distraught, with genuine circles around her eyes beneath the painted ones. Between her paleness and the rice powder, her face is as white as a plastered wall, with a wound in the middle, which is her mouth moving.

"There's still time to change your mind and to get something else ready," says Cussirat, whose lack of confidence is not diminished by how the sworn conspirator looks.

Pepita, suddenly, comes to life, like a marionette. She shakes her backside, her neck, her arms, and declares stridently:

"I want to dance! I want to dance! I want to dance a tango with Manuel Belaunzarán, for this is the happiest day of my life!"

Malagón turns happy, launches into an Aragonesque *jota*, and exclaims:

KILL THE LION!

"That's the way to talk, beautiful!"

Ángela, burying her concerns in the depths of her soul, says:

"Of course you're going to dance, and you're going to save your country, but first take a calmative."

Cussirat's heart hits rock bottom.

Ángela opens a cabinet, takes out a bottle, and from the bottle an eyedropper, and puts three drops of the calmative into a glass of water. They are watching how the poetess drinks the solution when don Carlitos, in tails, stunning, comes on the scene, rubbing his hands and saying in jest:

"What are you up to? What kind of plot is this?"

Before the mirror of his La Chacota house, assisted by his mustachioed wife and Sebastián, the Black, Belaunzarán puts on the bulletproof vest, the shirt, the shirtfront, the winged collar, the black tie, the pants, and, upon donning the tuxedo vest and trying to button it, realizes that it will not close.

"Damn! It doesn't close!" he exclaims in frustration.

Doña Gregorita, who has stepped back a few paces and is contemplating him as though he were a statue, advises:

"Wear the uniform."

Belaunzarán grows impatient.

"What the devil! You expect me to go to this party dressed in a military uniform? Don't you realize what this tuxedo signifies? Me, in the Moderates' household, dressed as a Moderate. It means, from now on, I'm not only the leader of the Progressives but also of the Moderates. The Parties are over and done with, I'm king of the island. Well worth the risk. So, off with the armor."

Sebastián and the wife, docile, help him take off the pants, the tie, the winged collar, the shirtfront, the shirt, and the bulletproof vest.

# xx. Everybody Dance

In the Berriozábal's vestibule, Ángela and don Carlitos greet the Rolls Royce Gonzálezes, who have just arrived. After kisses on both cheeks and the shaking of hands, don Bartolomé, reeking of Vetiver, and doña Crescenciana, on whose breast the pearls and warts are displayed as in a store window, link arms.

"We'll see you in a little while," doña Crescenciana says to Ángela, taking leave of her with a wave of the fingers.

"With such a tremendous party," don Bartolomé says to don Carlitos, "you're going to get a tax exemption."

Don Carlitos, flattered, winks and reminds him:

"The card, don't forget it."

The Gonzálezes, fat and self-satisfied, start the march toward the main room, with their *carte de visite* held before them, arm in arm and bumping buttocks every three steps.

The Berriozábal's chauffeur, dressed up as an usher, in recently purchased livery with chains, stands in the doorway to the drawing room. He takes the card out of don Bartolomé's hand, turns to the drawing room's interior, and cries out:

"His Excellency, señor don Bartolomé González y Arcocha, and his most excellent wife, doña Crescenciana Céspedes!"

The party is just beginning and the middle room is half empty. From the doorway, the Gonzálezes greet their friends as though they have not seen them for months, are just back from Europe and were still standing on the deck of a transatlantic liner. Then they separate, and the husband, who owns mills, goes to join don Baldomero Regalado, wholesaler in groceries, don Ignacio Redondo, owner of warehouses, don Chéforo Esponda, owner of the Red Boot, and don Arístides Régules, who deals in bananas and coconuts. She, on the other hand, goes over to the chairs arranged in a circle and sits between doña Segunda Redondo, who yawns, and doña Chonita Regalado, who, from where she is sitting, casts a bitter eye at her daughters, who, on the other side of the circle and dressed in tulle, are laughing at something just said to them by Tintín Berriozábal, who for the first time has been allowed to stay downstairs for a party.

Quiroz, the orchestra leader, with a face of the newly dead, moves his arms sparingly, to the rhythm of the *Vals triste*, until the players are ready, and then, taking up the viola, begins to play his part. Pereira, in one of don Carlitos's old tuxedos and shoes that are falling apart, absorbed in the music, has no eyes for the guests, who are gathering, and makes his violin moan precisely.

Cussirat, abstracted, in the middle of a group of friends making a fuss over him, apprehensively watches Pepita Jiménez, who is seated, apathetically, on a chair, listening to Conchita's chatter.

Barrientos and Anzures, each with a glass of Port in his hand, make their way through the baldheads and, with an air of great mystery and in low tones, ask Cussirat:

"Do you have any orders for us?"

Cussirat, trying to show confidence, requests:

"Stay on the alert, and wait."

Malagón, meanwhile, who has installed himself in the dining room without being seen, eyes the lobsters, sea bass, galantines, dressed hams, and eats a *canapé* of *pâté*; he chokes as the usher cry resounds throughout the house:

"His Excellency, the President of the Republic, Field Marshal, don Manuel Belaunzarán y Rojas!"

The orchestra plays the Arepa national anthem.

With his mouth full and with one finger wiping his lips, Malagón, on tip-toe, goes to the door, opens it part way, and sees Belaunzarán, Cardona, Borunda, and Mesa, whose formal clothes do not suit them, entering the room, alongside their hosts.

Ángela, with great aplomb, as if she has spent her life at court, comes walking into the room, leading Belaunzarán, and presenting him to the *crème de la crème* of their guests, who after a moment's uncertainty, brought on by their total ignorance of protocol, end up forming a line in order to shake, among smiles and courtesies, the hand of the person they detest.

Pereira, from his music stand, watches the operation most respectfully. Cussirat goes out onto the terrace and, taking out a small pistol, unloads the bullet and reloads it again. He is startled when he sees the door open and two figures come out of the house, whom it takes him a moment to identify as don Ignacio Redondo and don Bartolomé González.

"They say he has a great sense of humor," don Ignacio remarks.

Don Bartolomé glimpses Cussirat.

"Halt! Who goes there?"

"Friend! A man of peace," Cussirat answers, putting away the pistol.

"Pepe Cussirat! And what are you doing out here? You've already been presented to Belaunzarán?"

"I've already met him," Cussirat says.

Don Ignacio and don Bartolomé, sedate and conciliatory,

approach him, both thinking, and for good reason, that they noted a touch of rancor in his words.

"Come on, my friend, this is the time to forget quarrels!" don Bartolomé says.

"For the sake of the country," adds Redondo, who is a foreigner.

"Go on, my boy, go greet him. Coming from one of the oldest families, you'll please him immensely," González says.

"Not as old as his," Cussirat says, and, showing off his Darwinism, adds: "They've been around here since they were monkeys."

The old men laugh uncomfortably. Redondo settles matters: "Don't say that, Belaunzarán is a Biscayan name."

Cussirat, to get away from a pair of old fools, heads for the door, crosses the music room, deserted and in shadow, and reaches the main room at the moment when the orchestra begins to play a waltz, and Belaunzarán, with the gallantry learned in a brothel, goes over to the lady of the house, bows reverentially, and offers her his arm, and before the glassy stares of the guests, leads her into the center of the room, where he puts one arm around her waist, and begins taking little hops. She, who is an admirable dancer, follows him to perfection.

The young people dance, the old men move to the table with the wines, the old ladies to the chairs, and Pepita Jiménez, who fits in none of those groups, first leans against a doorjamb and then sits down on a chair upholstered in brocade.

Cussirat despairs. He walks across the room toward the wine table where he meets Anzures, his cheeks rosier than ever, smiling beneath his impeccable mustache, enthralled by the party.

"The party's turning out well."

"It would be better if El Gordo danced with who he's supposed to," Cussirat answers. "Waiter, a glass of Port."

Observing his boss's dissatisfaction, Anzures puts on a Lenten face. Cussirat turns to look at the dancing. Ángela, turning in Belaunzarán's arms, looks at him intermittently. Cussirat gestures to her with his eyes and one finger, indicating Pepita Jiménez and meaning "Get her to give him the eye." She nods. Don Carlitos approaches Cussirat.

"How's it seem to you, Pepe? You've seen a lot and you know. Isn't it a great party?"

"One of the best and, of course, the best ever given in Arepa," Cussirat answers, putting aside his bad humor for a moment.

"You think so? You really think so?" asks don Carlitos, thrilled.

"I swear it."

Don Carlitos, set at ease in society, recalls ancient guiles of the pimp:

"And you, aren't you ashamed? What are you doing here? Getting drunk, while that delightful girl, that angel, sits there"—pointing to Pepita. "Come on, you silly ass, right this minute I'm going to put you where you deserve to be. Or, better said, where you don't deserve: in pure heaven."

He takes Cussirat's glass away from him and pushes him toward where Pepita Jiménez is sitting, managing things so that Cussirat has no choice but to ask her to dance. The minute he holds her and they take a step, the music stops. Pepita looks at him, in ecstasy. Cussirat, taking advantage of the situation, walks her over to where Ángela and Belaunzarán are standing.

"Marshal," Cussirat says, "I've not had the pleasure of greeting you."

They both extend their hands, stiff, but amiable.

"How are you, Engineer?"

"I would like to present to you señorita Jiménez, my fiancée. She's a great admirer of yours."

Belaunzarán, gallant, kisses Pepita's hand. Ángela tops it off: "She's an admirable poetess."

Pepita, almost fainting from bashfulness, smiles. Belaunzarán looks at her without knowing what one says to poetesses. Ángela, understanding the situation, asks him:

"You're not interested in poetry, Marshal?"

Belaunzarán, frank, replies:

"I rarely have time to read it. But they tell me it's very interesting."

Ángela, indicating Pepita with her hand, says:

"Well, here you have our great authority. She can speak about poetry for hours."

The orchestra starts to play a fox trot. Belaunzarán bows toward Pepita, and says:

"I shall have great pleasure in chatting with you, at some other time," then, directing himself to Cussirat: "It's been a pleasure, Engineer," and, finally, to Ángela: "Señora, if you will grant me the honor."

And, taking her in his arms, off he goes, dancing the fox trot. Cussirat, screwing up his courage, takes Pepita and dances with her. Pepita, who is one of those people who *feel* music, moves her feet in a singular rhythm, which has nothing to do with her companion's, looks at Cussirat, enthralled, and tells him:

"You said I was your fiancée. Thank you!"

Cussirat stops dancing, releases his companion, places his outstretched palm in front of her, and says:

"Give me the pin."

Pepita, understanding that she has exasperated him, removes the pin from her décolletage, and hands it over, dramatically contrite. Cussirat puts it in his pocket, takes Pepita in his arms again, dances with her, leading her, discreetly, toward the edge of the dance floor. Pepita, glum, says to him:

"Now you're angry with me. What are you going to do with the pin?"

"Give it to Ángela. If Belaunzarán wants to dance with her all night, she'll be the one who has to do the job."

They have reached the edge of the dance floor. Cussirat escorts Pepita to the nearest chair, gestures for her to sit down and, when she obeys, he goes away without any civilities, leaving her, abandoned, sitting between empty chairs.

Cussirat approaches the chauffeur-usher, who, unoccupied, is watching the dance from the doorway, with all the pride of an artist, as though only his shouts could have made this party possible.

"When this piece is over," he orders him, "tell the señora that there's an urgent message for her, here, at the door."

"Very good, señor," the chauffeur says.

The chauffeur begins circling the dance floor, readying himself to be near Ángela when the music stops.

Cussirat, from the doorway, sees how, at the end of the piece, the chauffeur makes his way through the couples to reach the place where Ángela and Belaunzarán are standing and they, in turn, move toward where Pepita Jiménez is sitting. Then, he sees, anguished, that the three are talking, that the chauffeur comes up to them and says something to Ángela, who excuses herself to the others, separates from them, comes toward the door, and that, when the orchestra strikes up a bolero, Belaunzarán dances with Pepita. Ángela comes alongside Cussirat, all smiles.

"We've managed it!"

Cussirat is furious with himself.

"I'm an idiot! I just took the pin from Pepita—to give it to you!"

Ángela looks at him in horror, and utters the harshest phrase of her life:

"Damn it!" Then she collects herself and adds: "All right. Everything can be arranged. Give it to me. I will pass it back to her during the next break."

Cussirat hands the pin to Ángela, and she heads in Pepita's direction, dodging, with notable skill, the people who approach her in order to congratulate her, to ask her for a dance, etc. When the bolero ends, Ángela catches up with Pepita, who is with Belaunzarán and, pretending to caress her, puts one arm around both shoulders, and with the other hand takes Pepita's and gives her the pin, at the same time that she is asking Belaunzarán:

"How do you like our poetess?"

Belaunzarán bows, twisting the ends of his mustache:

"Charming. You won't believe it, señora, but she has enlightened me."

While Ángela is talking, Belaunzarán, very quickly, casts his eyes around, finds Cardona, who is at the edge of the dance floor, standing guard, attentive to the slightest of his boss's needs, and signals for him to come over. Ángela, meanwhile, has been saying:

"We ought to invite you some day to one of our Wednesday literary soirées. I'm certain it would interest you, Marshal. Don't you think so, Pepita?"

Pepita, putting the pin on her décolletage, says:

"At the very least, we will do everything possible to interest you."

At this moment, the orchestra plays the first chord of a tango. Ángela says:

"I'll leave you."

But before she can withdraw, Cardona arrives and, with a stiff bow and a bitter voice, says to Pepita:

"May I have this dance?"

Pepita becomes unsettled and responds:

"I'm dancing with the Marshal."

Belaunzarán, dripping gallantry, says to Pepita:

"I'm accused of despotism, but not egotism. It wouldn't be fair to deprive poor Cardona of the pleasure of dancing with you"—and then, directing himself to Ángela, he says: "Señora, will you do me the honor of consoling me?" and offers her his arm.

Ángela, destroyed, accepts and falls into Belaunzarán's arms, and he pushes her around the floor, expertly, to the rhythm of the tango. Pepita and Cardona also dance, reluctantly, with no sense of rhythm, looking into each other's face with frozen smiles.

Cussirat, with tensed lips, livid, puts a hand to his brow. From the other side of the dance floor, Barrientos sighs in relief, seeing that the danger has passed. Paco Ridruejo and Anzures, discreet and optimistic, come over to Cussirat.

"Everything's turned out to a T," says Paco Ridruejo.

"He didn't say a word," Anzures says and adds, addressing Malagón, who's approaching, his face full of puzzlement: "You spoke the truth when you said he'd excuse a pin prick."

"I thought the effect was quicker," says Malagón. "Could I have made a mistake with the substance?"

Cussirat, impatient, breaks the news to them:

"Nothing's happened yet."

The three men look at him, astonished:

"But, didn't she dance with him?" asks Ridruejo.

"Clearly she did," says Anzures, "I saw them."

"It was pointless," says Cussirat. "She didn't have the pin."

"And why didn't she have it?" asks Malagón. "Since I gave it to her."

"But I took it back from her," Cussirat says.

"Damn," says Malagón.

"Where is the pin, then?" asks Ridruejo.

"Pepita has it."

"Didn't you just say she doesn't have it?" asks Anzures, exasperated.

"I sent it back to her with Ángela," explains Cussirat feeling like an idiot.

"Damn!" Malagón says again.

"We're like the man who sold the cow," Anzures says, resorting, in his fury, to a peasant saying.

"What happened?" asks Barrientos, who just then comes up and joins the group.

Paco Ridruejo tries to explain, patiently, but unsuccessfully.

Cussirat, his gaze lost among the couples dancing, reflects. The other four look at each other, disillusioned, disturbed, and alarmed at the prospect of having to intervene directly in the assassination.

"What do we do now?" asks Paco Ridruejo.

"Well, get the pin back from Pepita and give it to Ángela," says Anzures, full of impatient authority, "because El Gordo isn't going to dance with the skinny woman again."

The others look in discomfort at Cussirat, thinking that he is going to take offence because they called his fiancée skinny. But he is not annoyed, and says:

"The whole plan's badly conceived. We're letting ourselves be influenced by what a foolish woman read in a novel. Why does it have to be while dancing? Between dances somebody can go up to Belaunzarán, give him a jab, and leave on the run."

The others look at him, terrified.

"I, of course, will not do that, because I'm a man without a country," says Malagón.

"Nor me, because I'm bad on my feet," says Barrientos.

"Nor me," says Anzures, looking at Cussirat reproachfully, "because there have been lots of blunders. The one who committed them ought to take the responsibility."

Paco Ridruejo says nothing.

Cussirat, annoyed at Anzures, tells him:

"Don't be afraid, don Gustavo, no one's asking you to do it. I'll do it myself."

This said, leaving the others absorbed in heated whispering, holding useless glasses, Cussirat starts walking to where Cardona, with frigid courtesy, is depositing Pepita in a chair.

She watches his approach, remorsefully.

"Give me the pin," says Cussirat for the second time.

Pepita places her hands upon her chest, protecting the décolletage, and then pleads in a heroic voice:

"No, Pepe. This is my mission, let me complete it."

Seeing her so determined and understanding that he cannot struggle with her in the middle of the room, Cussirat changes his plan:

"Don't wait for him to ask you to dance, get close to him and jab him."

Pepita stands up, with her hands still over her breast and then, after giving Cussirat a look of total surrender, begins walking, like a lamb being led to slaughter, among the couples crowding the floor. She has not walked three meters when the orchestra plays a waltz. She remains standing there, in the midst of the turbulent couples, like someone crossing a river, hopping from stone to stone, and surprised by a flood when half way across. Cussirat rescues her, coming alongside her, taking her around the waist, spinning her around.

Cussirat, his eyes fixed on Belaunzarán's pachyderm back, leads Pepita with undeniable skill and in dizzying turns toward a point at which the trajectories of the two planets—Belaunzarán and Ángela, Cussirat and Pepita—ought to converge. When the collision is about to occur, he orders Pepita:

"Now, bury it in him!"

He realizes in horror that Pepita has been *dancing* in her lover's arms, not moving herself in circles toward her fate or toward the accomplishment of her mission. When Pepita realizes that Belaunzarán is close by, it is because he is already far off, charmed, taking turns, dance after dance, with the hostess. Cussirat, livid with rage, looking into her eyes, says:

"Idiot!"

Pepita moans, cries, breaks away with magnificent repulsion from her partner and, disconcerting couples, causing them to collide, pushing and shoving, she clears a path for herself and exits, running out of the room.

Cussirat pursues her, furious, but he loses her. He sees her disappear into the music room. He races after her, dodges the faces, full of grotesque cordiality, of doña Chonita Regalado and doña Crescenciana González, who wish to speak to him, goes into the music room, and goes out on the terrace, which is deserted.

He looks around. The garden is dimly lit with some paper lanterns that Ángela, in a moment of *chinoiserie*, had decided to hang from the trees. He sees something move. Stepping into the artificial jungle, he calls: "Pepita!" and is startled when the greenery comes alive, with the flight, like that of frightened animals, of several couples who had been making love.

Cussirat loses his way in the garden's dark confines, calling: "Pepita!"

# xxi. The Party's Over

Pereira, enjoying his rights as an employee, sitting in a chair made of pear and apple wood, with his violin resting at his side, accepts the plate offered him by a servant, who does not know whether to treat him like the guest of previous times or like a musician hired for the night. He gets ready, calmly, to gobble up the lobster, drain down the champagne, and, from his place on the bandstand, watch the crowd, which like a herd, closing in on a watering hole, deliberately, but fatally swallowed up by the dining room door, behind which can be heard the noise of plates in collision with knives and forks, all submerged in the murmur of a thousand conversations that are not brilliant but sometimes have the virtue of splitting someone's sides with laughter. Through that same door emerge, with plates heaped high, groups of guests who recognize that the crush is too thick in the dining room and so seek refuge in the spacious, semi-deserted drawing room, taking seats that only a little while before were set aside for old ladies and wallflowers.

Cussirat, agitated but flawless, comes through the door into the room with the telephone and crosses toward the dining room when, spotting Pereira, he changes his direction and goes toward him.

Noting the approach of someone he admires so, Pereira chokes.

"Have you seen señorita Jiménez?" Cussirat asks, without paying any attention to the cough of the man he has questioned. "I've looked for her behind every bush in the garden, on the floor of the music room, among all the people in the dining room, in the bathrooms, I went into the kitchen to ask the staff, I called her house to ask if she'd come home, I've asked the guests—all to no effect."

"I saw her go upstairs," Pereira says, "but that was quite a while ago."

Cussirat, forgetting to say thanks to Pereira for his information, is at the point of mounting the stairs when Ángela, from the dining room doorway, calls him. He joins her, on the way passing don Chéforo Esponda and don Arístides Régulez, who come out of the dining room, each with plates piled high, after speaking with Belaunzarán, and commenting:

"He's a splendid fellow!"

"Terribly intelligent."

Ángela says to Cussirat:

"We've lost a magnificent opportunity. There were so many people around the table that nobody would have realized who jabbed him. Where's Pepita?"

"I've been looking for the last half hour, and I can't find her."

Ángela, concerned, brushes her hand across her face.

At that moment, with one eye on his plate and the other on the passing backsides of some girls, Belaunzarán comes out of the dining room, between Barrientos, don Bartolomé González, and don Carlitos, all smiles and affectations, as befits new allies.

"... I think it will be good for the country," González is saying, who up to this minute has never before thought of the country.

"Hypocrites!" Ángela comments under her breath.

Belaunzarán, seeing Ángela, nods, smiles, and says:

"This is all so delicious, señora."

Ángela, hypocritical, also nods her head and says:

"I'm glad you like the food, señor Mariscal."

"A bottle of *Blanc de Blancs* for el señor Mariscal," don Carlitos orders the *maître d'hôtel*, who is at the other end of the room.

The four men move off, talking about shady deals.

"If Pepita doesn't show up, I'll have to shoot him to death," Cussirat says, looking at the well-built back of Belaunzarán, who has stopped to speak with don Ignacio Redondo.

"Pepe, I told you, I don't want any bloodshed. Besides, you'll get yourself in a fix," Ángela says.

"If we don't finish him off today, we're not going to see him for months."

Doña Chonita Regalado and Conchita Parmesano come out of the dining room.

"Have you seen my daughter Secundina?" doña Chonita asks.

"No. Have you seen Pepita?" Cussirat asks.

"No," doña Chonita replies.

"Tintín isn't anywhere to be seen either," Conchita says to Ángela with a knowing air.

Ángela becomes concerned.

"Who knows what that rascal might be up to!" she says, and goes looking for him in the garden.

Doña Chonita and Conchita go up the stairs. Cussirat, still in the room, looks at Belaunzarán, at that moment sampling the champagne; he puts his hand to his chest, and then into his tuxedo pocket, moving the pistol from one place to the other. With his hand in his pocket, a determined gesture, and a robotic step, he approaches the muscular back of his victim, who is laughing at a joke that don Bartolomé has told him.

He does not reach his destination. Conchita Parmesano, altered, comes down the stairs, goes over to Cussirat, and stops him, with her hand on his arm and these words:

"Pepita has committed suicide."

Cussirat stands there, looking at her, stupefied.

"Go on up, she's in Ángela's bedroom," Conchita says and makes her way into the dining room, in search of Malagón.

Cussirat casts one last look at Belaunzarán's back, turns halfway, and ascends the stairs.

In the hall on the second floor he meets doña Chonita, cuffing her stupidest daughter's ears and asking her senseless questions:

"What were you doing up here, and what were your panties doing in that brat's hands?"

When she sees Cussirat, she shuts her mouth and disappears, pushing her daughter, into don Carlitos's bedroom.

Ángela's bedroom lies in shadow, illuminated only by a bedside lamp. Tintín, with Secundina's panties still in his hands, is looking, fascinated, at Pepita Jiménez's spread-eagled body, which lies upon the lady of the house's dignified bed.

In the same spot where they stood at the start of the party, in the vestibule of the house, Ángela, hiding her worry, and don Carlitos, ignorant of the fact that there is a dead poetess on the second floor of his house, say good-bye to Belaunzarán and his companions. Belaunzarán kisses Ángela's hand and tells her:

"It was a very enjoyable evening, for many reasons, but you, doña Ángela, were the principal one."

Ángela smiles. For a moment, her vanity as a hostess stifles her humanity and her patriotism, and she forgets, not only that there is a corpse upstairs but that the reception was, from the start, planned in order to take the life of someone who, unscathed, stands in front of her, saying thank you.

## XXII. Intermission

Pepita Jiménez was buried in consecrated ground, thanks to all their lies and the death certificate, provided by Malagón, on which he recorded the poetess's death as having resulted from cardiac arrest.

"She had been ill for a long time," he went around repeating everywhere.

The burial was solemn and well attended. The best of Arepa was there. In front of the open tomb, Padre Inastrillas extolled the deceased's fine qualities.

"This speech made much more sense than what Malagón said at don Casimiro's wake," Conchita Parmesano remarked to doña Crescenciana González.

Actually, both homilies said almost the same thing, except that to this Padre Inastrillas added some Latin phrases taken from the funeral Mass, and he appeared more imposing, in cassock and surplice with a lot of lace, than had Malagón in his old suit.

Pepe Cussirat, in strict mourning, with his eyes lowered and one hand to his brow, played the role of the inconsolable fiancé. The young ladies of Arepa, looking at him and wanting to nab him now that he was free, whispered:

"Oh, he looks so handsome in black!"

The married women commented:

"Obviously he feels her loss deeply."

Conchita Parmesano thought to herself:

"If these people knew that he killed her with his indifference!"

Actually, they were not long in finding out, because once the woman was interred, Conchita Parmesano could not resist the temptation and began to find fault with the cardiac-arrest version.

"I was the one who found her dead, and it was very strange," she kept saying.

With time, Pepita was destined to pass into Arepan social mythology as the first suicide.

"Don't write poetry," mothers warned their versifying daughters, "you see what happened to Pepita Jiménez."

And the story was told again and again of that woman who spent thirty-five years writing poems, ignored by men, and ended up by killing herself over disappointed love.

As a result of the incident between Tintín and Secundina, the girl, the stupidest of the little Regalado sisters, was submitted to a medical examination performed by Dr. Malagón, who, the longer he looked, the less he could find of anything inside the eldest girl that vaguely resembled a virgin and, after giving his opinion to the mother, went off to tell everyone:

"That girl's had years of practice," said Malagón, after dinner at the casino.

Doña Chonita spoke with Ángela, telling her that, given their children's being found *in fraganti*, it was only right that they be married. Ángela flatly refused.

"After she seduced my son, she still wants to marry him?" asked Ángela. "What nerve!"

From that moment on, the Regalado sisters never set foot

in Ángela's house, nor did the Berriozábals in the Regalados's. When the ladies met, they did not greet each other; when don Carlitos entered the casino, Coco Regalado left, saying:
"The old geezer who rapes women just came in!"
For, by some strange mental mechanism, Coco Regalado had come to the conclusion that don Carlitos (who never learned anything about what had happened in his wife's bedroom that night of the dance) was the one who raped Secundina, and not Tintín, as actually happened. In the beginning it seemed that Puerto Alegre society was going to split in two: those who visited the Berriozábals and those who visited the Regalados; but since the Berriozábals had better taste as well as more money than the Regalados, the latter ended up being isolated, without visiting or being visited by anyone, to the point that Secundina had to marry, years later, the olive salesman, who, according to the general consensus of Arepan society, was a yokel.

On the political scene, neither the death of Pepita Jiménez nor the Tintín-Secundina incident clouded the glory of the Berriozábal's dance honoring Belaunzarán in their own home, nor did those events impede the Parties' *rapprochement* or slow down the unfolding of events.
On the first of August, Belaunzarán named, as he had promised, three new deputies: don Carlitos, don Bartolomé, and Barrientos. On the 15th of August, punctually, the Moderate Party, in plenary session, named Marshal Belaunzarán Candidate for the Presidency of the Republic. On the 20th, the Chamber approved the Law of Ratification of Patrimony, by ten votes to none, and the Law of Expropriation passed from the file of PENDING PROJECTS, into the file of REJECTED AS IRRELEVANT. Finally, on the 1st of September, and only two months before the election, don Carlitos moved for the Chamber to

create the office of President for Life, a motion that was approved unanimously. With that passage, all the promises that Belaunzarán and the Moderates had mutually pledged over dinner at the La Chacota villa were fulfilled.

After the second plan's failure and the death of Pepita Jiménez, Cussirat, who did not want to receive any more condolences, dedicated himself to sports.

Some mornings he got up at dawn and went with Paco Ridruejo to hunt hares. They came back after dark, weighed down with bloody wild animals, and dined sumptuously on shell fish and domestic animals brought in from the English Hotel. Other mornings, he got up early, breakfasted on fish, went to the Ventosa Plain in the borrowed Citroën, and took a turn in the Blériot; sometimes he went alone, sometimes with Paco Ridruejo, and sometimes with Garatuza. Ángela, despite Cussirat's invitations, never wanted to go up in an airplane. In the afternoons, he mounted a horse, or fished, or went to visit Ángela. Evenings, before going to bed, he read one or another of the novels he had found in his grandfather's ancient, tiny library.

With Pepita's death, the conspiracy disintegrated. On being elected deputy, Barrientos said to Ángela:

"What we planned is forgotten. I'll remain silent as a tomb."

When the Law of Ratification of Patrimony was approved, Anzures told Ridruejo, using still another of his bovine images:

"Once the cow's dead, the fight's over, and it won't be me who wants to tear down the shed, now that everything's settled."

He never again stepped inside the Berriozábal's house and began going to the casino, where he played cards with González and Redondo.

Malagón confessed to Cussirat:

"As for me, with the risks I ran, I consider myself satisfied."

Cussirat, Ángela, and Paco Ridruejo, on the other hand, went back into action the day the Presidency for Life was approved.

# XXIII. Small Game

"As for killing Belaunzarán, we're in agreement," Paco Ridruejo said. "When and where's the problem."

They are in the music room, drinking tea.

"And, above all else, escaping," says Cussirat. "Because running the risks is one thing, going to a certain death is another, very different one."

They discuss everything, from bombing La Chacota with the Blériot to stabbing him in his private office.

"I don't have the courage for that," says Ángela in regard to the latter expedient.

They decide to kill him on the road to the San Pablito cockpit. Belaunzarán never misses a fight, which take place on Tuesdays and Saturdays.

"It'll take two bombs," says Cussirat, who has been reading, in secret, a treatise on explosives. "One for the gunmen's car and another for Belaunzarán."

Three men are needed, two to toss the bombs and one to drive the Citroën, because they are going to attack while the car is in motion. After turning down various candidates, they come to the conclusion that the driver has to be Garatuza.

"We'll explain to him what it's all about," says Cussirat. "I'm sure he'll agree."

"And what do I do?" asks Ángela, who wants to be useful.

"Nothing less than hide us," Cussirat tells her. "The attack will come at night, and we have to spend it somewhere. There's no point getting out alive, only to go killing ourselves in a plane crash."

They decide to kill Belaunzarán, spend the night at the Berriozábal's La Quebrada estate, not far from Ventosa, and to flee at dawn in the plane to Corunga and there request political asylum.

That night, Cussirat asked his servant if he was willing to drive the car on "a dangerous mission" and then to flee the country.

"If you take me with you, I'll do it with pleasure, señor," says Garatuza, who is not very happy in Arepa.

Villa La Quebrada is near Puerto Alegre, amid green ravines. More than using it for business, the Berriozábals view the villa as a relic of the origins of the family fortune. It was there that don Tomás Berriozábal, who at the start of the nineteenth century gave up trading in slaves, considering it unprofitable as well as dangerous, settled down, and dedicated himself to growing coffee, with such good results that his descendants forgot all about the slavery episode in their history and recalled him, for more than a century, as a coffee planter.

But time smoothes everything over. The Berriozábals, by means of advantageous matrimonial alliances and other ruses, went along acquiring more interesting and productive properties, such as Cumbancha, and left La Quebrada in the hands of administrators. Finally, at the beginning of this century, they went to live in Puerto Alegre, on Paseo Nuevo, attracted by electric lighting, English bathrooms, and the society of people of quality. This move, paradoxically, marked a return to La Quebrada, because nowadays (1926), they are in the habit, at two or three days' notice, of sending one of their men with orders for the administrator to open up and sweep out the main house, shake the dust out of the furniture, and slaughter a couple of suckling pigs, because the family, along with guests, is coming to do some shooting at the bottom of the ravines, and to give a blow-out in the galleries, overlooking the nearby hills, the field-workers' shacks half a mile away, and, in the distance, like a fine blue line, the sea.

A week after the Presidency for Life was approved, one of these hunts took place, attended by don Carlitos, wearing, for the first time, leggings that had recently arrived from Harrods; Ángela, with a tweed skirt that turned out to be too bulky; Cussirat, gotten up, impeccably, in the latest style from Kenya, topped off by a broad-brimmed hat with a jaguar-skin hatband; and Paco Ridruejo, in borrowed boots.

For two hours, the field workers and their women had listened, with admiration not exempt from fear, to the splendid racket of the guns going off in the depths of the ravines and, filled with curiosity, they came out of their houses to watch the boss, don Carlitos, pass by, suffocating and sweaty, fanning himself with his pith helmet, followed by a servant carrying a dead hare in his hand.

Ángela, Cussirat, and Paco Ridruejo, who had other interests and had climbed up another path, are already back at the house, opening doors and looking into spacious rooms with their solid, not very comfortable furniture, hand carved in mahogany by slaves.

"It's a good hide-out," Cussirat says.

"In the pantry there's enough preserved food for two weeks, and I'll send out some cans and bottles of wine," Ángela says. "I'll tell the administrator that there'll be guests and that he shouldn't mention it to my husband because that would be like proclaiming it in the public plaza."

"Ángela," says Cussirat, laughing, "it's only for a night, we're not going to live here."

Ángela disregards that argument. She does not like the idea of her guests being in want. Besides, in something so dangerous, you never know what might happen.

"What I don't like," says Ángela, referring to Barrientos, Anzures, and Malagón, "and seems unfair to me, is not informing the others. After all, they're involved too."

"If we can handle the business between Paco, my servant, and me, why inform the others? Why increase the risk of a gaffe?"

"It's just that since we invited them to begin with, we can't pass over them now without offending them."

Cussirat, to put an end to the matter, adopts an air of authority.

"Ángela, I'm the boss. Please: not a word to anyone."

Don Carlitos's voice is heard in the vestibule, saying:

"What kind of a joke is this? Where the devil did you come up, leaving me behind?"

Ángela, all smiles, goes to welcome her husband at the door. The others follow her.

"Did you have any luck?"

"A dog's luck. Forty shots, to kill one hare."

"Pepe got a wild boar."

Don Carlitos looks, envious, at the bleeding boar hanging between two posts on the terrace. He plays at being furious:

"That's the one that got away from me! Damn it! Besides leaving me behind, they take the best game away from me. Pepe, you scoundrel, I'm not inviting you again."

The other three laugh heartily. Don Carlitos drops into one of the rocking chairs near the door and says to his wife:

"All right, Ángela, you do the honors, have them bring us some sangría and something to stave off the hunger."

Bent over the spread-out map, around the dining room table, Paco Ridruejo and Garatuza get their final instructions from Cussirat.

"If the cockfight begins at eight thirty, Belaunzarán's car has to go around the Rotonda del Trueno no earlier than five after eight and no later than eight fifteen. We'll station ourselves at that point at eight, faking a breakdown, so as not to arouse suspicions. From there, we'll see them coming three minutes before they reach the Rotonda, which will leave us time to close the hood, take off, and cut them off there. They always come in two cars, one with gunmen and the other with Belaunzarán. Martín drives, Paco's in charge of the first car, and me of the second. Then we go to La Quebrada."

He looks at the others with artistic satisfaction and, seeing that they trust him and that there are neither questions nor things to discuss, Cussirat rolls up the map and says:

"Tonight's a full moon, and the sky's clear, so we can do this job without any mishaps."

Paco Ridruejo, with a bomb in his hand, mimes pulling the fuse and hurling it at an imaginary object.

# xxiv. Big Game

When Belaunzarán wants to go into the center of Puerto Alegre, he leaves La Chacota by Avenida Rebenco, reaches the Rotonda del Trueno, and turns down Avenida de los Carvajales; if he wants to go to the San Pablito cockpit, he leaves La Chacota by Avenida Rebenco, reaches the Rotonda del Trueno, and turns down Avenida de los Carvajales; if he wants to go to Guarándano, where he has an estate and a mistress, he leaves La Chacota by Avenida Rebenco, reaches the Rotonda del Trueno, and turns down Avenida de los Carvajales. Because only one street passes in front of the La Chacota villa, Avenida Rebenco, which stops at Rotonda del Trueno, where only one other street exits, Avenida de los Carvajales. All this in open country.

Under the *trueno* tree, which gives the rotonda its name, by the light of a full moon, Martín Garatuza opens the Citroën's hood and makes as though he wanted to adjust the motor, which is in perfect condition. In the back seat, bones atremble and butterflies in their stomachs, Cussirat and Paco Ridruejo light cigarettes. It is eight o'clock.

At La Chacota, meanwhile, Japan's first ambassador to Arepa, Horushi Tato, who presented his credentials the day before, who dined with the president, who is invited to the cockfight, and who has as his principal mission finding a way to erase the map for the Panama Canal, bows ceremoniously before Belaunzarán and gets into the black Studebaker, lent to him, which he is using while awaiting his Rolls at the Shuriku Maru.

Belaunzarán, sighing in relief, climbs into the presidential Studebaker, along with Cardona, Borunda, and Mesa. The gunmen's car takes the lead, followed by the ambassador's, and, finally, bringing up the rear of the procession, as befits a good host in the lands of the Indians, Belaunzarán's car.

Martín Garatuza, making out headlights in the distance, closes the hood and gets into the driver's seat, trembling.

"There're three cars!" he says, taking off.

"Damn! We have to decide. There're two possibilities left to us: go back home and wait for next Tuesday or run the risk of being chased by an intact car." Cussirat pronounces the fateful words:

"No changes. You after the first one, and me after the second," he orders Paco Ridruejo.

The Citroën, its engine bolting and tires bouncing, races along the dirt lane named Avenida de los Carvajales, in the direction opposite to the procession of cars, takes the curve around the Rotonda, leaves Belaunzarán's car behind, catches up with the Japanese ambassador's, and Cussirat, without having time to distinguish who is inside, pulls the bomb's fuse and throws it into the interior.

Harushi Tato has time—an instant—to see the bomb bounce in front of him, before its flash blinds him, and his guts spill out.

The bomb tossed by Paco Ridruejo has better luck, after getting off to a bad start. It does not enter the gunmen's car, as planned, but bounces off the hood, falls to the ground, lets the ambassador's car pass over it, and explodes a moment later, under Belaunzarán's car.

Belaunzarán, Cardona, Borunda, and Mesa have not yet recovered from the surprise and fright caused by a madman's passing them at full speed, and fall headlong when the chauffeur brakes violently, realizing that the ambassador's car is exploding a few meters ahead; then they rise a meter into the air, knock heads, hit against the roof, fall to the floor, and have to get out on the run, realizing that something is burning their backsides and igniting the car seats.

Confusion reigns in the gunmen's car. After a moment, when they were on the point of doing their duty and chasing the Citroën, they stop to see why the presidential car as well as the Japanese ambassador's are in flames, and, finally, its four occupants give contradictory orders to each other:

"Get out and see what's going on."

"Let's get out of here."

"Follow that car."

"Put it in reverse."

The confusion ends when the presidential Studebaker's doors open and out come, from each door, running like a rabbit, a terrified politician. This action clarifies the situation. The gunmen's car shifts into reverse and takes off in order to lend assistance.

Fortunately for them, Cussirat, through an excess of zeal, makes their job easy. The Citroën goes racing, at full speed, down Avenida de los Carvajales, on route to La Quebrada and the salvation of its occupants, when Cussirat, who is peering out the back window, sees the figure of Belaunzarán, illuminated by the flames, giving orders, and he then makes the most important decision of the night:

"Let's go back and finish him off."

Without hesitating, Martín Garatuza stops the car, throws it into reverse, and goes back toward the rotonda at full speed. Cussirat takes out the pistol and cocks it.

KILL THE LION!

Belaunzarán, his hat twisted, tie askew, trousers smoldering, but recovered from his fright, has taken charge of the situation. He points to the mangled metal of the ambassador's car and the inert mound that lies amid the wreck and, giving no heed to the little flame encircling the gas tank, gives a command to his companions, who stare back at him in terror:

"Get the Chinaman out!"

At that moment and as though to increase the confusion, a car pulls up and stops five meters from Belaunzarán. Taken by surprise at first, the marshal then calms down. He has recognized, leaning out the back window, Engineer Cussirat. Belaunzarán raises his hand in affectionate greeting, forgetting, for the moment, the air force episode.

"Engineer, help us!"

He stands frozen upon seeing that Cussirat, instead of helping him, takes out a pistol, aims at his belly, clenches his jaws, and fires six times.

For some seconds, both men look at each other incredulously: Belaunzarán at the dandy firing at him, Cussirat at the marshal who does not collapse. Belaunzarán's jacket fills with holes, through which pour, instead of blood, little clouds of dust, as though someone were beating a carpet. Before Belaunzarán recovers from his bewilderment, Cussirat recovers from his and, scared, pulls his head back in and orders:

"Let's get out of here!"

Martín Garatuza obeys. The Citroën takes off racing toward Carvajales, once again toward La Quebrada, the plane, Corunga, political asylum, and salvation. But now followed, very closely, by the gunmen's car.

Belaunzarán, believing that he is wounded to death, takes off his jacket and shirt, both full of holes, and the bulletproof

vest, and looks at his intact belly. The men surrounding him
tell him, on seeing his alarm:

"You haven't got anything, Manuel."

Belaunzarán looks at them scornfully:

"You think getting shot doesn't hurt?"

# xxv. One Jump Ahead

Obeying no logic except that of panic, Garatuza drives the Citroën across the country, bouncing along at full speed, without headlights and, without knowing it, toward the San Antonio dump.

"You can't see them now," reports Paco Ridruejo, who is leaning out the window in back.

Cussirat sighs, relieved. The car reaches the small village, travels along dark lanes, frightening dogs, following its vague, aimless route, when, coming to a corner, it collides with the gunmen's car.

It is not a big crash. No one is hurt, but the cars are out of commission for the time being.

The gunmen get out first, from fear, a bang on the head, and surprise, and the one with the Thompson opens fire on the Citroën. The first round leaves Garatuza and Paco Ridruejo riveted to their seats. Cussirat, unharmed, jumps out, on the run down the narrow street, bounds over a fence, falls in the midst of pigs, takes cover among scrub brush, leaps over another fence, runs through an empty field, crosses a stream bed filled with foul water, passes in front of a church, thinks he recognizes a market, reaches a wide street, and grabs a streetcar.

Seated among fast-asleep, swaying Blacks, he looks down and, by the light of the small bulbs, sees his shoes full of mud, his trousers torn, his hands trembling, and he passes one of them across his steaming brow, still hearing in amazement the loud panting coming from his parched throat.

"Good evening, Engineer," says a voice.

Cussirat raises his eyes. In front of him, hanging onto a celluloid grip, trembling to the car's rhythm like a marionette, Pereira looks at him with polite astonishment. Cussirat slides over in the seat, leaving space beside him. He looks at the violinist, full of emotion, reaches out his hand and, recalling his name for the first time, says to him:

"Pereira. God brought you here."

Pereira sits down, flattered, and questions him with a pause. Cussirat looks around for spies and sees nothing but indifference and the gallows faces of poverty. He speaks to Pereira in a low voice:

"I need you to hide me."

Pereira blinks.

"They're chasing me. It's a matter of life and death."

"Come to my house," Pereira says.

"Who do you live with?"

"With my wife and mother-in-law."

"Are they discreet?"

Pereira looks at him for a moment before answering, then shakes his head no. He sees how Cussirat sinks into despair, looking down at the streetcar's creaking floor. Pereira also looks at the floor, thinking he is going to find a solution to the problem there.

"There's a shed where the orchestra rehearses. Nobody sleeps there."

"Can I spend the night there?"

Pereira nods yes and says proudly:

"I have the key."

Cussirat puts his hand on his arm and says:
"Thank you."

Coronel Jiménez, Chief of Police, arrives in an open car at Rotonda del Trueno at nine P.M.
"Did you catch him?" Belaunzarán asks.
Learning that in the car they had chased there was one dead man and another wounded, neither of them Cussirat, Belaunzarán gives very specific orders:
"Mesa, a telegram. Condolences to the Emperor of Japan, signed by me. Borunda, to the cockpit: don't let them start until I get there. Jiménez and Cardona, with me to Ventosa. We have to cut off the retreat of that..." and he says something terrible about Cussirat.
Like a slumbering animal, ignorant of its impending sacrifice, Cussirat's Blériot rests peacefully, its gas tank full, on the plain of Ventosa.
Like a bellowing beast, spitting fire from its eyes, Jiménez's car, with its load of bad-tempered passengers, leaps ahead in the moonlit night, toward its defenseless prey, followed by a chorus of rabid dogs.
Riding up alongside the plane, Belaunzarán, his eyes glassy, gets out of the car and orders Jiménez:
"Give me the pistol."
Jiménez, in his anxiousness to obey, gets the weapon tangled in his cartridge belt, and when he manages to extricate it, after a struggle, hands it to his boss.
Belaunzarán empties the gun into the plane.
The Blériot does not collapse, but gasoline, like blood, starts pouring out of the holes.
Belaunzarán, his rage calmed by the shots, turns to Jiménez and orders him:

"Set it on fire."

Jiménez salutes him military style and turns to the sergeant who serves as his driver, and in turn orders him:

"Set it on fire."

The sergeant salutes and answers:

"Very good, Coronel, Sir."

He approaches the plane, strikes a light, brings it close to a wing, and the match disappears amidst the flames.

Belaunzarán briefly contemplates how the sergeant is setting fire to the plane. Then, satisfied, he turns to Jiménez and Cardona, who are watching the sacrifice, terrified, and tells them: "Let's get going to the cockpit. I'll drive."

That night Pereira was like a mother to Cussirat. He opened the dingy room, lit the oil lamp, pulled a bed together from benches, making it up with an old tarpaulin and some palm leaves, while the other man, exhausted, seated on a stool, watched him work. Finally, Pereira went to a nearby dive and bought some fish soup, which the sportsman devoured in his hideout.

"You won't be very comfortable," Pereira says, while the other man eats. "There's no pillow."

Cussirat sets the plate aside and confesses:

"Tonight, Pereira, I tried to assassinate the president. I didn't pull it off, and he recognized me. I don't dare go near the airplane, because by now they must be guarding it. I don't know what happened to the other two men who were with me. They must be dead. If they catch me, they'll kill me. I have to get off the island, and I don't know how I'm going to do it."

Pereira is stupefied. Cussirat asks him, finally:

"Now do you understand my situation?"

Pereira nods yes.

"If you think you ought to hand me over, go to the police

and tell them where I am. I won't put up any resistance, because I don't have the strength to defend myself. On the other hand, if you help me, you'll run the same risk I do."

Pereira stands up, full of generous impulses.

"How could you think, Engineer, that I'd inform on you? You can stay here until Thursday, totally confident that no one will see you. Thursday we have rehearsal, but by then we'll find another solution. Count on me, Engineer. I'll bring you food and a pillow and clean clothes, and even a bed, if you like."

Cussirat, moved, begins to cry silently, and seeing him cry, Pereira cries, too.

When Cussirat lays his head upon his jacket, doubled over as a pillow, and closes his eyes, waiting, anxiously, for sleep that is not going to come, Pereira puts out the lamp, goes out of the shabby room, locks the door, putting on a padlock, and putting the key in his pocket, starts walking toward his house, going over, with pleasure, certain details, saying to himself:

"How could you think I'd inform on you, Engineer...? Count on me, Engineer ... We already have found a solution ..."

At the cockfight, Belaunzarán has bad luck.

When he sees his cock dead in the ring and wads of bills escaping from his hands and ending up at other end of the pit, he cannot stand it any more, and, red in the face, almost apoplectic, he rises from his front-row seat, enters the ring, picks up the dead bird and, taking a bite out of its neck, tears off its head.

"Long live Belaunzarán!" shouts the crowd, seeing its idol spiting out the neck and wiping off his bloody mouth with the back of his hand.

"Where were you?" asks Esperanza from the bed, seeing her husband enter the room.

"Don't question me," says Pereira energetically, "because I'm not going to answer."

He comes alongside the bed, and in a single pull yanks off the sheet, uncovering his wife, naked and trembling, who closes her eyes and implores:

"Don't hurt me!"

In the dark, Pereira and Esperanza look toward the ceiling, without being able to see it.

"Galvazo had to leave," Esperanza remarks, and pauses a bit, before continuing. "They came to look for him from the police station," she lets another pause elapse. "They had a prisoner they had to question."

Pereira, without blinking, goes on looking toward the dark ceiling. Esperanza yawns, turns over in bed, her back to her husband, and is fast asleep. Pereira repeats in his mind:

"What do you think, Engineer? You think I'm going to inform on you?"

# XXVI. They don't Know what to Do

Cussirat turns over on his hard, creaking bed and looks at the shapes the stick wall sketches in the moonlit night.

Outside, dogs howl.

Inside, mosquitoes buzz.

Cussirat sweats. He watches how a rat creeps in through a crack, crosses the room, goes out through another, and is chased, unsuccessfully, by a hunting dog. He is thirsty. He gets up, and groping, with great difficulty, finds the pot that Pereira filled with water. He takes it in both hands and drinks eagerly. When he is drying his mouth, gasping, he realizes that there is a roach floating in the pot. He almost vomits. When he collects himself, he goes back to his bed, and lies down moaning, as if he were gravely ill. He, Cussirat, had been on the verge of swallowing a roach! He is unable to get back to sleep.

A century passes. Suddenly a strange noise startles him and causes him to sit up. Something moves outside the dingy room. Through the sticks he makes out a threatening silhouette. He hears the roar of a prehistoric animal. He hears a dull thud against the wall, and the building shakes and seems about to fall down. Cussirat gets up, greatly alarmed, and takes out the pistol. The beast roars again. Cussirat laughs. It is a hog, scratching its back on the sticks. Cussirat lies down again, calmer, and while the building is being rocked by the hog, he sinks into a sea of nightmares.

Cussirat opens his eyes. The room has been transformed. Light pours in through the cracks. He is refreshed. The mosquitoes have disappeared. Outside, jumbled noises are audible. Cussirat gets up, goes over to the wall, peeks through a crack, and sees how an enormous sow is running away, chased by her litter, all wanting to attach themselves to her nipples. Some bald hens mince by daintily and with no special destination, moving their head, nervous, as though expecting the worst.

From the hut next door, a thin Black woman, with a torn dress and a tangle of hair hanging loose, comes out, tosses a fistful of corn on the ground, and calls:

"Chick-chick, chick-chick, chick-chick..."

The sow and the hens sniff up to the corn and fight over it. The Negress goes into a corner of the enclosure, lifts her skirts, and squats.

At that moment, Cussirat realizes that a gaunt, young dog, its ears pricked up, is wagging his tail and looking up at him, eyes shining.

Pereira, with a mysterious air, opens the chest of drawers and chooses his best undershorts, best undershirt, and a dress shirt, with brown stripes, that once belonged to don Carlitos. He puts these three garments into his briefcase, goes to the dressing table and, after thinking about it, also puts in his straight razor and a half-used bar of soap. He stands looking, sadly, at the soaking wet towel that Esperanza has left, twisted, on a chair, and closes the briefcase.

The article, when it appeared in *El Mundo*, turned out to be the most sensational of the year. Better even than when MODER-

ATES ATTEMPT TO BLOW UP PALACE. One dead, one wounded, one fugitive, two cars demolished, the ambassador from Japan blown to bits, and a plane incinerated.

The article almost gave don Carlitos a fainting fit at the breakfast table, and he got indigestion from his cup of chocolate.

"And I, who presented Pepe to the president! And you, who invited him to the party! And the two of us, who took him hunting on Sunday! We're in a tight spot, Ángela! How did this madman not understand that we would be the first to be injured by his atrocities?"

Ángela does not respond. She cannot take her eyes off the second headline: ENTIRE POLICE FORCE HUNTS FUGITIVE.

When Anzures learned that Paco Ridruejo was wounded and in the hands of the police, he fled to his country estate.

"They'll loosen his tongue," he thought, "and we're going to pay, the innocent for the guilty."

Barrientos, cleverer, took refuge in the English Embassy, with two changes of clothing and a letter of credit for a cool million.

"Apples or oranges," he told Sir John, in English, "I'm sailing on the *Navarra* when it gets in."

Malagón, who read the news at the Steamboat Café, went to see Ángela in a rented cart, thinking:

"This is the end! If I run away from here, where do I go?"

He did not find her in. She was out at La Quebrada, searching for Cussirat and receiving the administrator's bad news that "the guests had not arrived."

Disconsolate, she got into the car and went back to Puerto Alegre. She went to see Malagón but did not find him, because he was still running around looking for her. At the Bank of Arepa they told her that Barrientos had left by stagecoach. She did not even go to look for Anzures. Finally, she met up with Malagón, at twelve thirty.

With his face soaped up, moving the straight razor as Pereira shows him, Cussirat shaves himself. When he finishes, he says:

"I'd like you to do me a favor or, rather, one more favor."

"Do you want a mirror? I'll bring one tonight."

"Still another."

"Tell me."

"I want you to go to Ángela's house and tell her, without anyone else finding out, that I'm safe."

"Engineer, I will do that with pleasure."

Looking at himself in the fogged-over mirror in his bohemian room, Malagón, with the skill of ten years' practice, replaces the tooth that has fallen out, and fixes it there with Campeche wax. Ángela, tense, stands in a corner, looking at him.

"In this matter, we have to tread gingerly," Malagón says. "Any question may prove fatal. Worse if I ask it myself! That Pepe is in a jam, we already know. That they haven't caught him, we also know. The only thing we can do is to stay on guard, and read the newspapers."

Ángela suppresses an exasperated gesture. She realizes that it is useless to stay here and goes toward the door. Malagón prevents her leaving.

"Come on, Ángela, don't be like that! Do you want me to go out on the street, asking what happened to Cussirat ... or to go looking for him? The police are in charge of that. Besides, if I find him, who can assure us that Paco Ridruejo hasn't squealed on us and they're not tailing me?"

Ángela makes an effort to stifle a sob, without succeeding.

Malagón tries to console her with clumsy caresses on the cheek and shoulder.

"He may be dead," says Ángela, drying, with a certain impatience, her tears with a handkerchief. Then she regains her calmness. "He didn't come out to La Quebrada, as we had agreed."

Malagón looks at her steadily, and in one of his rare moments of perception, asks her:

"You love him a lot, don't you?"

She avoids the old man's look, and does not answer, but accepts the bamboo chair, broken-down, that he offers her. After a moment, Malagón, as if weary of the mute understanding that has been established between them, interrupts it with a torrent of conventional philosophy.

"But, let's see, what can be done? If something happened to him and the newspapers don't have any information, that's because the police don't want to give it out, and if the police don't want to give it out, that's because they probably have their reasons. And in that case, there is nothing to do, but to stay calm and patient, and sooner or later these things will be known."

Ángela wipes her nose with the handkerchief, and looks slantwise at the wall.

"I don't want to see him," Ángela is saying to the servant, when, coming into the vestibule, she encounters the person she does not want to see, seated on a chair. "Good afternoon, señor Pereira. I'm in a rush."

"One minute, no more, señora, it's urgent."

Ángela, faced with the inevitable, indicates for Pereira to continue, and goes into the music room, taking off her hat.

"Sit down," she says.

Since he does not obey her, she realizes that Pereira has changed.

"Engineer Cussirat sent me to tell you that he's safe."

For a moment, Ángela cannot believe that Pereira, whom she has so often looked at inattentively, is now giving her the news she has so longed for. When, finally, she accepts the situation, she crosses to stand next to him, takes him by the lapels, and asks in a low voice:

"You've seen him?"

He meets the excited look of his questioner, and tells her, without being able to hide his pride:

"Yes, señora. I have him hidden away."

Ángela frees Pereira's lapels.

"Is he injured?"

Pereira grows prouder and prouder.

"Nothing's happened to him."

Ángela sighs, relieved.

"Can I see him?"

Pereira ponders for a moment, then says:

"No, señora."

"Why not?"

"Because the Engineer has given me no orders to that effect. Probably, he thinks it's dangerous."

Ángela takes a moment to accept the situation. Then, with great determination, and always looking at Pereira fixedly in the eyes, she says to him:

"In that case, if you help me, señor Pereira, nothing will happen to señor Cussirat. We will get him out of Arepa safe and sound, cost whatever it costs. Even if it costs our lives. Can I rely on you, señor Pereira?"

Pereira, moved by the intimacy of which he is the object, and with a lump in his throat, replies:

"Count on me, señora."

Ángela looks at him with interest, and smiles at him in gratitude.

# XXVII. Nobody Turns down a Thousand Pesos

The Puerto Alegre Chamber of Commerce, whose president is don Ignacio Redondo, in order to stay on Belaunzarán's good side and, in a certain sense, to erase any suspicions that might exist of a connection with the attempted assassination or, at least, of sympathy with those who wanted to pull it off, offered "in a simple ceremony," conducted in the offices of *El Mundo*, the sum of one thousand pesos for any information that might lead to the arrest of Engineer Cussirat.

The following day, notice of the reward appeared in the newspaper, alongside a photo that had been taken of Cussirat on the day of his arrival, just descended from his airplane. Pereira read the notice in Cussirat's presence, before going off to teach a class at the Institute.

"Don't leave the building, Engineer," he advised him before leaving.

During the class, he shocked the students with his severity. He expelled Tintín Berriozábal with the warning:

"You have no reason to come back, because, as of now, you're failing this course."

Tintín went complaining to his mother, who, contrary to what he was expecting, put a stop to his protests, saying:

"I'm glad. And stop complaining, because I'm sending you

to the United States, to a military school, as a boarding student."

Tintín shut his mouth and don Carlitos never learned of the tragedy.

That night, in doña Soledad's living room, Pereira places the chessmen on the board and, from the tail of his eye, sees how Galvazo, who has just come in, hangs his hat on the boar tusks, crosses the room deeply depressed, and sits himself down in front of him.

"What's the matter?" asks Pereira.

"The canary died on us before he sang," says Galvazo, almost in tears. Never before has he looked so humane. Who could have imagined that he would feel so deeply the death of Paco Ridruejo?

Pereira offers his condolences and Galvazo reports the most sordid details of the demise.

"And now what are you going to do?" asks Pereira.

Galvazo shrugs his shoulders.

"The president really put his foot in it by burning the airplane! He's got us in a jam, because with the wounded man dead and the burned airplane, which was the only trap, there's nothing left for us but to hope the fugitive's alive and breathing," he grows more animated as he develops his reasoning, "and that's not so hard, because Engineer Cussirat isn't a man to die of age while in hiding. Sooner or later he's going to want to get off Arepa. And how's he going to get off Arepa? It's not as though there're so many ways of leaving Arepa. He has to go on the *Navarra*. And the *Navarra* docks tomorrow. That's where we'll nab him. What bothers me is that I, who wanted to contribute to solving this case, am left holding the bag, because the weakling couldn't take anything."

Pereira moves a pawn. Galvazo puts his hand on the knight but, before moving it, says:

"Now, there's another possibility. That somebody whispers in my ear. Because, after all, Pereira, in this country there's nobody, nobody, you hear me? who can resist a thousand pesos."

Pereira compresses his lips and shakes his head, with the expression of a philosopher who has heard a great truth.

Galvazo moves the knight, saying:

"There you go."

Both opponents, absorbed, look at the chessboard.

Pereira went with the story to Ángela: Paco Ridruejo died before talking, the *Navarra* is a trap, and in Arepa there is no one who can resist a thousand pesos.

Ángela, who, thanks to Lady Phipps, knew where Barrientos was, took her jewels from the dressing table, and with them in her handbag, went to get him out of the English Embassy. Barrientos, learning of Paco Ridruejo's silent death, gave up his political asylum and went back to everyday life, taking up his activities again with a one-sided deal: thirty thousand pesos in jewels worth a hundred thousand, plus Ángela's solemn promise that whatever happens, neither she nor Cussirat nor Malagón is ever going to say that he, Barrientos, had been present at that fateful dinner.

Felipe Portugal, owner of the sow and husband of the gaunt Negress, sings, in the moonlit night, on the shore of the sea:

> *I'm the happy fellow*
> *Who gets up singing*
> *With his bottle of wine*
> *And his cards in his hand.*

KILL THE LION!

Not very far away, within reach of his voice, also on the seashore, Cussirat and Pereira, stretched out in the sand, watch two Blacks hunting crabs and enjoying the fresh air.

"Friend Pereira," says Cussirat, "I am a washout. I tried to kill him three times. The first time, it cost the life of the Moderate Party; the second, of my fiancée, and the third, of my valet, who was one of the most extraordinary men I've ever known, as well as my great childhood friend. I, the one responsible, save myself, I come to be put up in a shed, I see poor people for the first time, I sleep badly, and discover that, after everything's said and done, the poor are going to go on being poor, and the rich, rich. If I'd been president, I would have done many things, but it wouldn't have occurred to me to give money to the poor. So, how much does it matter if the president's a murderer or not?"

"It never would have mattered to me," says Pereira, who has followed attentively this line of reasoning.

"You're wise," says Cussirat. "The worst of it," he continues, "is that I wouldn't dare to make another attempt. Because the worst fright that night gave me was when I fired six shots into Belaunzarán, and he didn't fall down. Now I understand that he must have been wearing armor, but that night it seemed like witchcraft to me. I'm not going to mess with that man again. And now I can't even recall why I wanted to mess with him in the first place. So now I don't have bad intentions. Unfortunately, it's too late. If I stay on Arepa, it's to die, and if I leave, they'll kill me . . . and the worst of it is that I don't want to die. I am a coward."

"No, Engineer, don't say that. You are the bravest man I've ever known."

Cussirat gets up and goes to skip pebbles into the sea; then, he comes back to Pereira and says:

"I am a coward, Pereira, because I don't even feel capable of defending myself or of doing something to go on living."

Pereira gets to his feet and says to him solemnly:

"Don't worry, Engineer. You don't have to do anything. Doña Ángela and I are arranging a way for you to leave here, and you can go live, very happy, somewhere else."

Cussirat looks at him for a moment, and repeats:

"I don't want to die."

Pereira, to console him, says:

"Remember, Engineer, in this country nobody can resist a thousand pesos."

# XXVIII. The *Navarra* Sails

But what Ángela lays down on Coronel Jiménez's desk is not a thousand, but fifteen thousand, and moreover, she says to him:

"These are for begging your mercy, Coronel. When I have proof that my friend is safe, I'll hand over some more."

"Señora," says Jiménez, taking the bills and stuffing them into the desk drawer, "I am a man of honor."

Ángela, who knows that she is dealing with a louse, smiles and says:

"It's not that I doubt you, Coronel. It's just that I don't have the money right now, and I need three days to get it. But I too am a person of honor, Coronel. Or are you going to doubt my word?"

Faced with the impossibility of collecting it all in advance, Jiménez opts for gallantry, in hopes of being paid some day, even if in kind.

"Señora, you can count on your friend's being able to get on board without mishap."

Ángela stands up. Jiménez, hastily because his visitor's movement took him by surprise, imitates her. Ángela extends her hand.

"When the *Navarra* arrives in La Guaira, Coronel, if everything turns out as we have agreed, I will receive a cable, and you the rest of your money."

Jiménez shakes Ángela's hand and accompanies her to the door, after struggling with a chair that has gotten in his way.

When she has gone, Jiménez hurries to the telephone and calls the palace.

"Señor Presidente, sir, I have news … My agents have discovered that Engineer Cussirat will attempt to board the *Navarra*, the day after tomorrow, at eight thirty at night. What are your orders?"

Belaunzarán, in his private office, telephone in hand, looking at the statue of himself, thinks, and then says:

"We're not going to do anything, Jiménez. This country can't put up with any more martyrs. Let him get away. Remove the guard at that hour."

"Very good, sir," says Jiménez, at the other end of the line, and hangs up the telephone, his eyebrows raised in amazement and a smile on his lips. Then he clasps his hands, at the height of happiness:

"Another fifteen thousand pesos!" he exclaims.

And, in a lavish outpouring of emotion, he breaks into a grotesque dance.

At five o'clock in the afternoon on the following day, the *Navarra*, making waves, sails into the bay of Puerto Alegre, carrying in the hold a shipment of wine, ordered by Belaunzarán and destined for the celebration of the coming presidential inauguration.

At the Redondo Department Store, don Ignacio, the owner, personally waits on doña Ángela, who is making a purchase that will stir up everlasting gossip in Puerto Alegre: gentleman's clothing that is not don Carlitos's size. Three light suits, a tuxedo, a raincoat, a cap for traveling, twelve English poplin shirts, and six neckties, which she herself carefully selects.

To all this she adds a book, *A Tale of Two Cities*, in an edition expurgated by the Church, and has everything sent by driver, in a leather suitcase, to the *Navarra*, with instructions for leaving it in Cabin A, which is the best on the ship.

"Don't you think this clothing must be for Cussirat?" Redondo asks señora Segunda that night.

The following day he goes to the police station to report his discovery, in hopes of saving himself the thousand pesos that has been offered as a reward. But they pay no attention to him, and drum him out, as though he were talking nonsense.

He will spend the rest of his life trying to explain this phenomenon to himself, without ever discovering the identity of Ángela's lover.

Out on Punta del Caimán, Pereira and Cussirat bid farewell. In the water, a few meters offshore, are the launch and the Black man who must carry Cussirat to the other side of the bay, where the *Navarra* is anchored.

Cussirat embraces Pereira and tells him:

"Pereira, I have nothing at all to repay you with for all you've done for me, but if you accept a little money, which is all I can give you, you'll take a load off my mind."

He takes out his billfold and the money in it, but Pereira rejects it:

"Not a centavo, Engineer. And rest easy, because, for me, the satisfaction of being useful to you is sufficient payment."

"I would like to give you something, something you'd like, but I don't have anything," says Cussirat, but, suddenly, he recalls:

"Oh no, yes, I have."

He takes out the pistol.

"I have this pistol. It's not going to be of any use to me any more. Would you like to keep it as a souvenir?"



KILL THE LION!

Pereira, fascinated, looks at the weapon, and takes it into his hands, like something precious. Cussirat looks at him, pleased.

"You really like it, don't you?"

Pereira nods yes and looks at him, grateful. Cussirat opens his arms:

"Give me a hug, Pereira. We'll probably never see each other again."

The two men embrace, moved. Then Pereira accompanies Cussirat to the rocky shoreline, and watches him jump nimbly into the boat.

The Black begins to row. The launch moves off. Cussirat, standing, looks toward shore, raises a hand in last farewell, and then turns around and sits down, looking ahead.

When Cussirat turns his back to him, Pereira looks down at the pistol in his hand, puts it away in his pocket, and again looks out at the silhouette of the launch moving away, navigating the calm sea, disappearing into the night.

Ángela, from her window, sees the *Navarra*'s lights slip into the blackness. Then she closes the window and touches her brow, pensive, satisfied, and sad, all at once.

The next day finds the *Navarra* sailing happily on the choppy sea.

Up on deck, Cussirat, wearing the traveling cap and overcoat that Ángela bought at the Redondo Department Store, reclining in a folding chair, is reading *A Tale of Two Cities*.

A feminine figure comes on deck, walks with some difficulty owing to the ship's rolling, reaches the railing, and bends, leaning on it, looking out to sea.

Cussirat leaves off reading in order to look at the woman. Discreetly, he shuts the book, gets up, and walks over to the railing, leans on it, looking out to sea, and out of the corner of his eye, at the unfamiliar woman's face. She is not bad.

# xxix. Several Triumphs

In the back patio of his mother-in-law's house, amid trash and furniture in a state of decomposition, Pereira points the pistol toward a target he has made for himself, and fires.

The neighbors, alarmed, say:

"Señor Violín has a pistol."

And they add, prophetically:

"One of these days he's going to kill us a chicken."

Esperanza and Soledad, terrified and full of reproaches, watch Pereira's practice from the kitchen door, covering their ears with their hands.

Pereira goes up to the target and looks for the holes, without finding any. Then, puzzled, he looks around, searching for the results of his shots, which he finds up in the bramble-covered fence.

"If you don't know how to shoot, don't shoot," his mother-in-law tells him.

Pereira, disappointed, goes into the house and puts the pistol away in the wardrobe.

In 1926, Arepa held the most peaceful election in all its history. Nobody voted, and the winner was the only candidate. When Belaunzarán received the news of his triumph, they were already uncorking the bottles and the suckling pigs were on the spit. Fifteen "intimate friends" attended the party, as *El Mundo* reported, among them don Carlitos, González, and Barrientos. The wives were not invited, and the men had a splendid night, as don Bartolomé told doña Crescenciana, who was waiting up for him in a bad mood.

On December 15th, exactly two weeks before the President for Life's Inauguration, which was to take place on Holy Innocents Day, December 28th, the *Navarra* sailed into the bay, carrying Guillielmo Ferrosso, an accomplished and famous French journalist, despite his name, who had already glorified Mussolini and who brought with him the assignment to write a series of articles for *L'Ilustration*, under the general title of *La lumière dans la Terre du Soleil*, which was to deal with progressive regimes in Latin America. For that reason, Belaunzarán granted an interview, in which he gave a summary description of everything his regime was *not* thinking of undertaking. He also let them photograph him in a broad-brimmed hat, hunting deer; in casual clothes, playing billiards; and dressed in white with a racquet in his hand, alongside a tennis court's net. The interviewer described him as a powerful man, with a firm jaw and a look that seemed to penetrate "into the beyond."

On Inauguration Day, Pereira got up early, dressed, put the pistol in his pocket, and before going out, alerted his wife, who was sitting naked, looking at herself in the mirror:

"Today I'm not coming home at midday to eat."

She grew distressed.

"You don't love me any more?"

"Yes, I do, but I'm not coming home to eat," he answers and goes out of the room before he is asked something else.

Esperanza remains there, her mouth half open, closing it only when she turns to look at herself again in the mirror.

From the sidewalk, Pereira, standing among the curious, watches as Belaunzarán, wearing a morning coat and riding in a landau, arrives at the Chamber of Deputies; sees him leave the Chamber, now wrapped in the nation's flag; follows the landau, in the midst of the uproar, along calle de Tres Cruces, toward the Plaza Mayor; sees Belaunzarán enter the palace, then appear a little later on the balcony and deliver a speech to which Pereira pays no attention.

Later, from a table at the Steamboat Café, he sees Belaunzarán ride by in his new car. Pereira returns to his house at five, disappointed, and hears news that lifts his spirits:

"Professor Quiroz came looking for you," Esperanza tells him, her face full of unformulated reproaches. "The orchestra is playing at the casino tomorrow at a dinner they're giving for the president."

Pereira smiles.

The Moderates, headed by don Carlitos, don Bartolomé González, and Barrientos give Belaunzarán a dinner to celebrate the triumph of his candidacy, his ascent to the Presidency for Life, and the harmony now reigning in Arepa.

At the table are seated, mingled together, rich men with pretensions to distinction and loutish politicians. Fourteen waiters, brought in from the English Hotel, serve the *hors d'oeuvres*, the soup *à la cressonière*, the pampano in butter, the chicken in almond sauce, the *boeuf bourguignon*, and the Dutch cheese—all washed down with tart wines that came in on the *Navarra* and made all the more enjoyable by the melodies played by Professor Quiroz's string orchestra.

Actually, neither the *boeuf bourguignon* nor the Dutch cheese were ever to be served, because when Belaunzarán was in the middle of the chicken breast, it occurred to him to ask:

"Have them play *Estrellita* for me."

As fate would have it, Quiroz, the first violin, did not know the song. Pereira, with the conductor's permission, came to the front of the orchestra, to play the first solo of his life, which was also to be the last. They say that he had never played so well. He played with so much feeling that tears came into the president's eyes. Belaunzarán liked the piece so much that when it was over, he put his hand in his vest pocket, took out a twenty-peso bill and signaled for the player to come over.

Pereira, with the violin and bow in his left hand, comes up to Belaunzarán, bowing his head and, accepting the bill with two fingers of his left hand at the same time that he puts his right into his breast pocket, takes out the pistol, holds it almost perpendicular over Belaunzarán's head, and, carefully, like someone squeezing an eye-dropper and counting the drops as they come out, fires six shots into the gentleman who has just given him a tip.

Belaunzarán fell flat on his face, into the plate, and stained the tablecloth.

The rich men, who were so frightened that night, took more than twenty-four hours to understand that it was going to be much easier to work things out with Cardona, the new President for Life.

After Cussirat's departure, Ángela dedicated herself, body and soul, to pious works, pouring into them a great part of the capital, ever more enormous, belonging to don Carlitos. In the afternoons, instead of playing music, she sits in her room discussing new plans with Conchita Parmesano and Father Inastrillas. On the wall, near the place where Pepita Jiménez died, hangs a framed photograph of Pereira—facing the firing squad, up against the wall, moments before dying—that today is sold, all over Arepa, as a postcard.